TALES OF AN 8-BIT KITTEN

A CALL TO ARMS

D0963708

Published in French under the title *Un Chaton Qui S'est Perdu dans le Nether
Tome II* © 2019 by 404 éditions, an imprint of Édi8, Paris, France
Text © 2019 by Cube Kid, Illustration © 2019 by Vladimir "ZloyXP" Subbotin

Andrews McMeel Publishing
a division of Andrews McMeel Universal
1130 Walnut Street, Kansas City, Missouri 64106
www.andrewsmcmeel.com

20 21 22 23 24 SDB 10 9 8 7 6 5 4 3 2

ISBN: 978-1-5248-5531-4
Library of Congress Control Number: 2019952465

Made by:
King Yip (Dongguan) Printing & Packaging Factory Ltd.
Address and location of manufacturer:
Daning Administrative District, Humen Town
Dongguan Guangdong, China 523930
2nd printing—6/29/20

ATTENTION: SCHOOLS AND BUSINESSES
Andrews McMeel books are available at quantity discounts with
bulk purchase for educational, business, or sales promotional use.
For information, please e-mail the Andrews McMeel Publishing
Special Sales Department: specialsales@amuniversal.com.

TALES OF AN 8-BIT KITTEN

A CALL TO ARMS

Illustrations by
Vladimir "ZloyXP" Subbotin

Andrews McMeel
PUBLISHING®

In memory of Lola Salines (1986–2015),
founder of 404 éditions and editor of this series,
who lost her life in the November 2015 attacks on Paris.
Thank you for believing in me.

—Cube Kid

"He's not waking up."

"Shake him, then."

"**You** shake him."

"**Why me?!**"

"What's his name, anyway?"

"Um, I think it starts with an *E*? **Eduardio?**"

"Hey! Eduardio! **Wake up!**"

These voices pulled me from a deep sleep.

When I opened my eyes, I saw three humans standing over me: two boys and a girl.

They were wearing the exact same **armor,** made of metal that was almost black, with hints of red and white.

"My name is **Eeebs,**" I said.

With a smile, one of the boys waved and shouted, "*Haiwoo!!*"

The girl sighed. "You **really** need to stop saying that, Leonardios."

"It's **Leo,** for one thing," he said. Like her, he couldn't have been older than twelve. "And what's wrong with 'haiwoo'? It's our official greeting!"

"There's nothing **official** about it," she said. "It's just a **stupid way** to say hello."

"Yeah, whatever. We'll vote on it soon."

After giving them a **puzzled look,** I glanced about the room.

1

Strangely, Breeze wasn't there. Her bed was **empty.** I vaguely recalled hearing a door close in the middle of the night, but I fell back asleep right after . . .

"Um, **where** is she?" I asked.

"No idea." The other boy stepped closer. He was the oldest of the three. He must have been sixteen. "The mayor asked us to come get you. It seems the villagers have their hands full. Some kind of problem, I don't know. Anyway, they want us to take care of you."

"**Us?**"

"Oh, sorry. I'm **Hurion Rubyshard.** And this is—"

"**Lylla,**" the girl said. "No last name."

"Leo, here. We're with the **Lost Legion,** like Kolbert. Haiwoo!"

HURION

LYLLA　　　　　　LEO

"You'll be staying in our **clan keep** for now," Lylla said. "Until Runt gets back, anyway."

"What will I be doing there?"

"Not much."

"Well, as long I don't have to work with the **angry man with the eyebrows,** sign me up."

Leo and Lylla exchanged glances.

"The angry man . . ."

". . . with the eyebrows?"

"**Drill** is this **villager** who . . . never mind." I took one last look around Breeze's bedroom. It made me feel a little sad.

That's how my day began: A **villager named Runt** was still nowhere to be found, and Breeze **vanished mysteriously** in the middle of the night, leaving me with three people from another world.

I looked at them again.

What do I do? Do I go with them? I'm pretty hungry. . . .

I checked my **inventory,** but I didn't find any food there. That was when I **noticed** the piece of paper. Breeze must have put it there right before leaving.

Eeebs,

I just learned that Runt was sent on a mission.

The mayor seems to think he needs more real-world experience.

But he should have come back by now. So I've been asked to go find him and bring him home.

Someone from the Lost Legion should be coming to see you this morning. It's best if you stay with them until I return.

Sorry for this. And please tell no one.

—Breeze

Well, that settled it.

And even without the letter, I would have gone. Because Lylla offered me a new food item—**baked pufferfish.** It must have had some kind of enchantment, because as soon as I ate it, Lylla and I became **best friends.**

"Do . . . do you have any more?"

"No," she said. "But we have more at the keep. I'm the best fisher in the **Legion,** and Steph is the best cook, so—**Hey! Where are you going?**"

I was already out the door.

(Of course, I had no idea where I was going,
so I stopped and waited for them.)

4

While we made our way to their keep, I asked a ton of questions. Not so long ago I was an ordinary and clueless **animal,** so asking tons of questions is **only natural.** What's a clan? Were all of them from Earth? Why were they wearing the **exact same armor?**

They were indeed from Earth, which made them **Terrarians.** And since I was born in **Aetheria,** that made me an **Aetherian.** (Although, I believe that's just a polite way of saying NPC.)

As for their black armor, that was the Legion's **official uniform.** It was only recently that their clan had obtained enough material to make a set for every member.

Of course, we drew a lot of attention as we walked through the streets. I mean, Hurion was really tall, he carried a **huge red sword,** and he had white and red hair. Meanwhile, Lylla wielded a sticklike weapon like the one **Greyfellow** carried. And Leonardios was so **excited** he was practically yelling. But despite their **strangeness,** I drew the most attention.

A villager woman glared at me and said, ˙**Go away!**˙

A little boy ran up to me. ˙My house was **destroyed** because of monsters like you!˙

˙**No monsters allowed!**˙ an elderly man shouted. He was carrying a stack of carrots in his arms.

"Move along," Hurion told them. "To interfere with us would be to interfere with the mayor himself. **This kitten** is under his protection."

This didn't help much.

"Kitten?" someone shouted. "You call that thing a **kitten?!**"

"Whatever it is, it's probably infested with void fleas!"

"No, he isn't," Leo said. "I already checked! What? Their wings are used in at least three different **brewing recipes!**"

"**Get out of here!**"

"I'll never trade with you **Legionnaires** ever again!"

"Ignore them," Hurion muttered. "Just keep walking. We don't need **any more . . . incidents.**"

Leo turned back to me. "Yeah, we've already had a few of those," he said. "Yesterday, this—" He wasn't watching where he was going and **slammed into** the man carrying an **armload of carrots.** The carrots went **flying everywhere.**

"**Sorry!**" Leo said, handing him **several emeralds.**

Scowling, the villager pointed at Leo and opened his mouth—but before he could speak, Leo handed him a red potion. "**Here! Take this!**"

This only made the man **angrier.** "I don't get why we still let you people in our village! Ever since you showed up, the **monster attacks** have only gotten worse!"

"**Fine!**" Leo gave the man twice as many emeralds as before, along with a blue potion and a ruby.

"You think you can just—"

A shout in the distance interrupted him. It was so loud they all turned toward it.

Drill was the **angry man with the eyebrows.** He was barking orders at some villager building a house. The villager must have made a mistake when putting in a door, because the man with the eyebrows got so angry he ripped the door off its hinges and wielded it like a weapon, slamming it against the wall of the house. He was shouting with each swing.

On the first swing: **"Cloud mining—"**

On the second: **"—thunderstorm jogging—"**

The third: **"—empty-bucket carrying—"**

The fourth: **"—GRAVEL-BRIDGE BUILDING—"**

On the fifth one, the door shattered into hundreds of wooden pieces.

". . . P-P-P . . . P-P . . . P . . . POWDER-KEG JOCKEY . . . !!"

Suddenly, Hurion seemed to understand who I meant by "the angry man with the eyebrows."

"Let's get outta here," he said. "He's been acting pretty strange, **more angry** than usual, and I really don't want to deal with him right now. Like, times a **googol.**"

"What's a googol?" Leo asked.

"A **really huge number.**"

"Oh."

7

We got out of there quickly.

Considering how the villagers were treating me, I was **almost glad** these people came to ~~find~~ rescue me. Really glad.

The Legion's keep was **underground.** After going down a long flight of stairs, we walked through a huge **cavern system,** with tunnels to the left and right. Each tunnel had a sign—Tunnel 74, Tunnel 75, and so on. Every so often in the middle of the main tunnel were signs that read "**Lost Keep**" and "**This Way,**" with little arrows pointing in the direction we were heading.

It reminded me of **the Nether.**

Me, sniffing an object called a "lever."

"I don't think I've ever seen a cave this big in my life," I said.

"Actually, **it's a mine,**" Lylla said. "And, yeah, **the tunnels** are getting pretty big, aren't they? All that **stone** had to come from somewhere."

"This whole main corridor used to be an **underground ravine,**" Hurion said. "Made things pretty easy for the villagers. All they had to do was make **new side tunnels.**"

Leo glanced back at me. "We'd been wanting to build a **Legion keep,**" he explained. "Lucie thought it'd be a good idea to build one down here, since it'd make a great hideout for all the noobs when we're attacked."

"Who's Lucie?"

"Our **Architect,**" Lylla replied. "She's an **expert builder,** so when it comes to construction, she has the final say." Lylla pointed at a large sign that had a map of the surrounding tunnels. "That's her **handiwork.**"

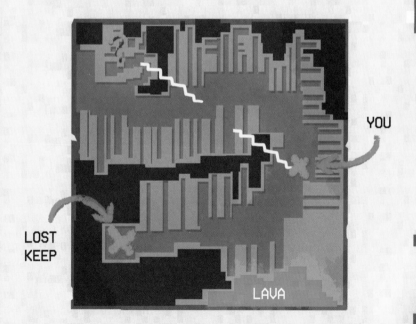

YOU

LOST
KEEP

LAVA

There were jagged white lines for staircases leading up to the surface. The dark sections indicated a type of **stone** called **black quartz.** The miners—villagers mostly—had recently found a lot of it. Like obsidian, black quartz is difficult to mine. There wasn't a single tool in Villagetown capable of breaking it. Even if there had been, mining it wouldn't be worth anyone's time. It was **pretty much worthless.** You couldn't craft with it, and it was about as **weak as dirt** when it came to explosions, so you couldn't really use it for building, either. Basically, black quartz is the bane of miners.

(I'm not a mining expert, by the way. Leo told me all that.)

"Oh, and see that tunnel?" he said. He pointed at the map and then down the corridor, to a tunnel on the left. "That's **Tunnel 67.** There's a branch that's **67b,** but it's sealed off, because it **leads to a dungeon.** So never go down there, all right?"

I blinked. "**Dungeon?**"

(Yeah, that's pretty much how all of my conversations were going lately. Someone would use a word or phrase I didn't understand, like "dungeon." Then I'd reply with that word or phrase as a question.)

"They're **dangerous places,**" Hurion replied. "Almost always underground and always **filled with monsters.** With you being a cat, I'm sure you'll go sniffing around at some point, but **don't go sniffing around** in there, okay?"

"Okay." I pointed at the question mark on the map. "What's that?"

"That's more of the **ravine**," Lylla said. "It goes on for quite some ways. The miners haven't really explored past the question mark, but they're planning to soon. They've already mined **every last block** of ore around here."

"Come on!" Leo said. "We're almost there! It isn't much, but we do have a **lava moat.** It was easy to make, since there's a lava lake not too far from here. Oh, and we have a **training golem.** It's like a monster, since it can move and fight back, but it doesn't do any damage. We don't have traps yet, but we will soon."

Hurion mentioned that it was still under construction. And, yeah, it did look unfinished. It was still the **coolest** house I'd ever seen, though. **I mean, keep.** Sorry.

Legionnaires were scattered everywhere around the front courtyard. Some were building. Others were carrying big red blocks, which Lylla said were **dangerous.** A few were attacking what looked like a **giant wooden monster.**

Clearly, everyone here was preparing for battle.

"Welcome to **Fort Noobery!**" Leo exclaimed. "The dining hall's on the left, and your room's on the top floor. Lylla will show you around. Oh, please make sure you get to sleep somewhat early. We haven't figured out how to enchant the doors so they stop making so much noise, and some of the guys can get a little cranky." He turned to Hurion. "**Come on! We gotta work on our Building! It's been days since we've had a skill increase!**" He waved at me, walking away. "Bye!"

"See you later, Eeebs," Hurion said before following Leo.

I turned to Lylla. "Is Leo . . . **always** like that?"

"He just got a new weapon. That puts him in a **good mood,**" she replied with a smile. "Okay, I'll introduce you to **Steph** then show you your room."

She took me into the keep. The interior was the same color scheme as their armor, either black or dark gray, with shades of red and white—**the Legion's clan colors.**

Obsidian blocks were **strategically placed** to contrast with the blocks of white quartz. The **members of the Legion** could come back to a place of luxury and comfort after a long, hard day of **defending**

12

the wall or **scouting the wilds.** A place where the **wonderful aroma** of enchanted food wafted from the keep's dining hall, each item prepared by Steph, who had a very high **cooking** skill.

"Hi, Lylla. I take it this is **Eeebs.**"

"**WOW,** you know my name? Earlier, Lylla was calling me Eduardio."

Lylla shrugged. "It's hard keeping track of names. So many **new recruits . . .** we've had a lot going on lately."

"We have," Steph said, **inspecting me curiously.** "And now it seems like I'll have to start working on some new recipes. Have you tried that **pufferfish** yet?"

"**Tried?** I think you mean **devoured,**" I said. "In fact, I was wondering whether you had any more."

"Sadly, I have only one left." She handed it to me. "They're hard to craft. Don't worry, though. I'll start on a few of the easier fish recipes."

"How do you know so much about cooking, anyway?"

"Well, I'm a **Baker,**" she said. "That's my **class.**"

13

"Class? You're a student?"

Steph laughed. "No, no. Class is another way to say **job** or **profession.** As a Baker, I can **craft food items** and dishes no one else can."

"Actually, everyone here has a class," Lylla said. "Including me. **I'm a Wizard.**"

I only became **more confused** when Steph added, "Some of us even have two classes. **It's possible to have up to eight,** although it's typically better to just focus on one when you're first starting out."

"Oh." I didn't fully understand. *(At this point, I barely knew what a sword was.)*

Steph turned back to her ovens. "Oops. My pies are done. **Gotta go.**" She waved. **"Nice meeting you, Eeebs!"**

I followed Lylla out of the dining hall, up the stairs, down a hall past some **grumpy guy,** and to my room.

Unlike the rest of the keep, there was **nothing special** about my room. It was just a **5 × 5 block chamber of gray stone**—no carpet—with a bed and a single chair.

"I could show you the rest of the keep," Lylla said, "but I have a feeling you'd like to explore on your own, since **you're a cat** and all." She glanced around the empty room. "You're free to decorate it however you like."

I stepped into the room and sniffed it. I'd never slept in a bed before and had no idea what it would be like. **"So what now?"**

14

"Take a nap," Lylla said. "Kolbert will come see you when he can. Do you have any questions, or . . . ?"

She hovered at the door. But I barely heard her. I was already drifting off. I was **pretty tired.** After all, I think I got only eleven hours of sleep the night before. Maybe twelve.

Lylla had told me to take a nap.
So I did. For five hours.
Cat problems, you know?

To be honest, I probably would have napped longer had the door not **burst open**. I **jumped so high** I not only hit the ceiling but also nearly dented the stone with my head.

In came five Legionnaires. One was wearing a bright outfit; the others were in clan uniform. They began introducing themselves.

"So **this** is the **terrifying cat?** I'm Cobalt."

"Me? I'm **Zain**. Nice to meet you, Eeebs. By the way, what level are you?"

"Hi, I'm **Becca**," said a girl with dark brown hair.

". . . **Rubinia**."

"FlamedGhost. People just call me **Ghost**, though."

FLAMEDGHOST

ZAIN

RUBINIA

COBALT

"Now we have a **super weird NPC quest**," Ghost said. "Villagetown is **so crazy**." He paused, studying me. "Wonder what kind of stats he has. Maybe we could turn him into a tank?"

Zain nodded. "We could use a tank. What did Ched say about him? **He's immune to fire?**"

I stared at them while they were talking, realizing that my original goal—**catching up with Runt, completing my quest, and heading to the capital**—was now on my list of things to do in the distant future.

But, hey, at least I didn't have to interact with the **angry man with the eyebrows.**

"What's a tank?" I asked.

The five of them exchanged a look.

"**Wow, he doesn't know a thing,**" Ghost said.

"I really don't," I admitted. "**I'm learning, though.**" To their astonishment, I stood up on my hind legs. Although awkwardly. "**See?**"

They laughed.

"All we need now is to get him a pair of boots," Becca said.

They laughed again. Why? What was the joke?

Becca

17

Well, Zain didn't laugh. He looked **kinda glum**. "I don't know much, either," he said. "In fact, **I barely remember Earth.**"

"Me either," Cobalt said. "My past life is **just a blur. . . .**"

"Same here," Becca said. "After I woke up here, it felt like I'd slept for **a thousand years.**"

"I heard of one player who can't even remember his own name," Ghost said.

Becca turned to him. "You mean **S**? You've seen him?"

"Nah. Sprinkles did. Tried getting him to come here, but he refused. Crazy dude's been leveling up since the **Cataclysm.**"

The Cataclysm?

It was all too much.

There were too many new people and too many new words. *(And what kind of name was Sprinkles?!)*

Cobalt seemed to sense my confusion. "Cataclysm . . . that's what we call **the day we arrived here.** Months ago."

"You mean the **Great Summoning?**" I asked. "That's like a thing mentioned in **the Prophecy.**"

"Whatever you wanna call it, **it's the day we all woke up here. In this world,** I mean. **Totally confused and scared.** Some even had a kind of **nervous breakdown.** They just stared ahead, not speaking, barely eating. Took 'em weeks to get right."

"How many humans . . . um, **Terrarians** were sent here?" I asked.

"Who knows?" Zain shrugged. "Thousands, maybe? We have no way of locating them. Nor any kind of long-distance communication."

"From what we know," Becca said, "there's at least a thousand of us. The majority of us are hiding, though. In the capital. They're refusing to . . . **play the game.**"

Cobalt laughed. "Good luck to them. **You need emeralds** to live in a place like that. **You can't farm in the capital. Or build your own house.** From what I heard, they're **basically homeless, begging the NPCs** for food."

"Begging?" a rather calm voice came from behind them. "I suppose they are. But who can blame them?"

It was **Kolbert, or Kolb**—the commander of the Lost Legion—standing in the doorway.

As he stepped into the room, he continued, "Since this world is no longer a game, even squaring off against a single low-level monster is no easy task. **Fear overtakes you, your stomach turns, your knees become slime, and when you take more than a single damage point, you forget everything you know.** So I understand why they refuse to play. But the Legion has no such option. **It's our duty to protect them.** And we won't stop until we have the resources to buy them proper homes and decent food."

For a moment, the other five were silent, as though stunned by his speech.

Then Rubinia made an **annoyed sound,** like psh. "You know how much a house in the capital costs? We're talking at least twenty thousand, and that's for a shack!"

"Then we'll build our own city," Kolbert replied. "And we'll defend it ourselves. Or we can escort them to one of the elven sanctuaries where they can at least farm. **No matter what, we'll find a way.**"

Ghost slapped him across the back. "I'm with you, brother! **For the noobs of Aetheria!**"

"You already know my feelings about that," Cobalt said before turning to Rubinia.

"Same," she said. "We really do need to start leveling up more."

"Guess I'm in," Becca said. "Going out of our way to **hunt real monsters** is a little nuts, sure. But hiding here is **total noobery.** I really can't deal with the villagers anymore."

Kolbert shrugged. "Unless you quit the clan, you're still going to have to 'deal' with them from time to time."

"He's right," Ghost said. "We can't abandon them. And, besides, this is a good location. We'll always use Villagetown as a base."

Zain looked at Kolbert. He **seemed embarrassed.** "I'll . . . do my best."

The Legionnaires all fell silent. Then Kolbert looked at me. "Hey, Eeebs. Sorry about all of this. The mayor—"

"They told me," I said.

"Oh." He moved closer. "Well, I agreed to take you in because I figured you're better off here. Plus there's a chance we might be able to learn a few things from you. You're clearly not a **standard NPC.**"

"Is that really what I am? An NPC?"

"Sorry, I should say '**Aetherian,**' because this world really does appear to be . . . **real.** So maybe we really were summoned here, as hard as that is to believe." Looking **quite exhausted,** he sat down in the room's only chair.

With him being so close to the torch, I saw that his armor had tiny specks of . . . **was that bright pinkish ooze?**

Zain noticed this as well. "**Cake slimes?**"

The commander nodded. "Yeah. Ran into a horde to the south. They seem to be coming out of that ravine."

(This was an opportunity to ask another question!)

"What's a cake slime?"

"Exactly what it sounds like," Becca said. "One part slime, one part cake. Probably the result of the **Eyeless One's** experiments."

"They're the **weakest monsters** of all time," Ghost added. "They are noobs. **Noob monsters.** Our scouts have been seeing a lot of them lately, in the south. The ravine Kolb mentioned is a few **biomes** from here."

Rubinia went for the door. "Well, I should go. So many items to enchant."

"I should take off as well," Cobalt said. "Still have a lot of building to do."

Becca followed them out without a word.

Those three didn't even say goodbye. The other two did, though, and left soon after.

However, Kolbert didn't move. "Mind if I crash in your room for a bit?" he asked. "Not too many know I'm here. I might be able to actually get an hour or two of **shut-eye** before I head out again."

"It's fine."

"Thanks." He sank further into the chair. "It's really tough being a **clan leader.** Everyone's always coming to me with some problem or asking for advice on something."

"Why not have more leaders?"

"Probably a good idea. But who'd be crazy enough to accept?"

"I won't pretend to understand how difficult it must be to manage a clan," I said. "**Especially in times like these.**"

". . ."

No response.

Before long, he was snoring lightly.

I curled up on my bed, trying to understand everything.

My quest to find the mysterious villager named Runt: **postponed until further notice.**

My quest to **learn more about the strange people from another world: proving to be quite challenging.**

Do they _really_ like sleeping in chairs?

Well, I'd slept for another three or so hours.

I was feeling **really exhausted** lately. Always sleepy, always yawning. Not sure exactly what was going on. It was the same feeling I'd once had back in **the Nether** shortly before I transformed into the thing I am today.

Thing. That's what people were calling me.

Not *Eeebs*, or *cat*, or *ocelot*, or even *cute little nether kitten.* Nope. Just **that thing.**

In other news, I explored more of the keep.

The second floor was filled with rooms for the **highest-ranking** members of the Legion. *(And me. Why? Who knows.)*

On the first floor, there was the dining hall, and to the east were long halls leading to more rooms. One was for enchanting, another for brewing. Then there was a **storage room**, a **crafting room**, a **forge,** and—in the very back—the **clan meeting room.**

Actually, I'll just draw it. Way easier that way.

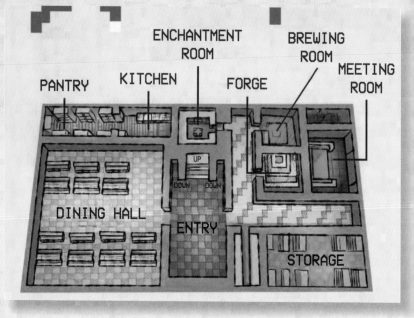

ENCHANTMENT ROOM

BREWING ROOM

MEETING ROOM

PANTRY   KITCHEN   FORGE

UP

DOWN   DOWN

DINING HALL

ENTRY

STORAGE

LOST KEEP FIRST FLOOR

I first entered the brewing room.

By "entered," I mean I just **pushed open the door and zoomed in.**

The three people inside **whirled** around when I barged in. One was so **startled** he drew his sword.

"**Hey!**" a girl with red hair snapped. "**Can't you see we're working?!**"

"You should learn how to knock," a girl with purple hair said. "Or at least walk in calmly like a normal person."

24

"It's fine," the boy said. "He'll learn." He smiled at me. "You must be Eeebs. I've heard so much about you. I'm **Krafty,** and this is **Amber** and **BlastLight.**"

". . . H-hi."

I noticed that the girl with **purple hair** had really weird ears. They were **large and foxlike.**

BLASTLIGHT   KRAFTY   AMBER

Then I learned that some of these people weren't human. Like Amber. She's a **foxtail**—three-quarters human and one-quarter fox. Don't ask me.

I'm <u>learning</u> as I go.

Leo was in the meeting room.

That room had a **large map** on the wall. According to Leo, we live on a massive expanse of land, called a "continent." The name of this continent is **Ardenvell** or **Eohune** *(pronounced "ee-yune")*.

EOHUNE

The Thorns of Ao
Ravensong
Corbois
Capital of Aetheria✖
Valley of Dawn
Villagetown
Algath
Mota
Hexgate
Evesse
Astres

Now here's the thing.

The map was made of **thousands** of tiny little squares.

Each of these squares is a biome. That's a square section of land thousands of blocks across. Each biome is a different type. Plains, forest, savanna, mountain, swamp, taiga . . .

Why am I explaining this?

Well, each biome is around twenty thousand blocks across.

So this world was huge. **Really huge.** So huge it was impossible for me to get my head around it.

This continent had two names. The most common was **Ardenvell,** but those who lived in the capital preferred to call it **Eohune.**

After telling me about all of this, Leo laughed. "Guess this makes me your first official teacher, right? I wonder what I would have said if someone had told me, months ago, that I'd eventually be living in a large clan keep with a bunch of random kids in another world, teaching Aetherian geography to a **cat-monster** named Eeebs. . . ."

I laughed, too.

After all, my own life has taken a **rather strange turn.** Not so long ago, I only thought about chasing butterflies.

The last room I explored was **the forge.**

Kolbert was in there, standing over a large chunk of iron, pounding on a sword with a hammer.

When I asked him what he was doing, he grinned. "I'm repairing. To properly defend this place, we have to take care of our gear."

"Is . . . **gear** really so important?"

"It is. **Without gear, you won't have decent stats.**"

"Stats?"

"Like strength, agility, crit chance, crit damage, attack speed, armor. **The more stats you have, the stronger you'll be.** The easiest way to raise your stats is by wearing gear with enchantments."

I showed him my claws. "I'm already enchanted, though."

"Yeah, I heard about the **rune chamber.** The thing is you'd be even stronger if you were wearing a full set of items." He pointed to his armor. "Items like these."

"Um."

I almost laughed at the thought of dressing up like one of them. I tried picturing myself wearing a tunic, trousers, shoes. **No way**—even if it would provide more "stats."

"That reminds me," Kolbert said. "The mayor said you have a status screen?"

"You mean visual enchantment."

"Actually, we call them **status screens,** or stat screens for **short.** Anyway, can you open yours?"

Nodding, I focused on the word **"ability,"** like I had several times before. My abilities screen appeared in the air before me.

"You really do have a ton of stuff," he said. "How about your **attributes?**"

"Um . . ."

Attributes, I thought, assuming that was how I accessed them. The abilities section suddenly **fell away,** revealing:

ATTRIBUTES +3

 STRENGTH   DETAILS

 AGILITY   DETAILS

 VITALITY   DETAILS

 INTELLECT   DETAILS

 RESOLVE   DETAILS

 KARMA   DETAILS

Attributes are like . . . a measure of your strengths in certain areas.
I guess that's a horrible way to describe it, and I can't exactly remember everything Kolbert told me.

First, there's strength (or **STR**). That doesn't need an explanation. The higher your strength, the more damage you'll do with **melee attacks.** (*And most physical abilities. Like a claw ability or something. Those are called "techniques."*)

Agility (**AGI**) is how **nimble** you are. The more AGI you have, the faster you can **attack, move, and use abilities.**

Vitality (**VIT**) is a measure of **life-force.** Higher VIT gives you more health and increases your **resistance to illnesses that affect the body,** like **disease** and **poison.**

Intellect (**INT**) mainly affects how many **skill points** you gain at each level and the **effectiveness of magical abilities,** also called **spells.**

Resolve (**RES**) is like your **inner strength, mental fortitude, willpower.** It affects **energy regeneration,** along with resistance to abilities that affect the mind, like **Sleep, Charm, and Fear.**

Finally, there's karma (**KAR**). It's a **mysterious force** that affects how **lucky** you are and **influences your interactions with other people.**

(*My INT was 10 because of Higher Intelligence. Each level of that ability provides 2 INT.*)

"What's the +3?" I asked.

"That means you have **three attribute points,**" Kolbert said.

"You can tap that square, then tap any of your six attributes, and it'll go up by one. But once you do, you won't be able to change them later, so choose carefully."

"Hmm . . ."

After considering each attribute again, I decided to put all three points into **VIT.** Kolbert suggested vitality, as the **more I have, the greater my chance of survival is.** I wasn't gonna argue with that.

My **health bar,** in the lower left corner of my vision, increased slightly. It grew by half a heart, meaning **I'd gained +1 health.** *(I would gain more health from this later, as my health would increase every time I leveled up, and that increase is affected by VIT.)*

Oh, and 0 is totally average, while 255 is approaching that of a **godlike being.** And the numbers can go into the negatives: −50 or lower is like a **slime.** *(Or like me after anything less than sixteen hours of sleep.)*

"Think of these numbers as percentages," Kolbert said. "If one's strength is 50, they'll deal 50% more damage, and −50 strength would mean 50% less damage."

"How do I gain more attribute points?"

"Every time you level up, you'll gain three."

"And I level up by . . . **defeating monsters.**"

"Yep. You could think of **XP** as part of a monster's life-force that you absorb. The stronger the monster, the more XP you'll get. Completing quests also gives you XP in the form of crystals."

"Got it. Oh. How do I see how much XP I have?"

"One way is switching to your class screen," he said.

Kolbert then informed me about how the screens are kind of like a book. **Well, more like a stack of pages.**

The screen was showing my **attributes.** With the swipe of a paw, I could make it fall back, revealing the next screen. I could flip through them until getting to the **classes section.**

Alternatively, I could just think of the word "classes," and that screen would appear at the front. **That was faster.**

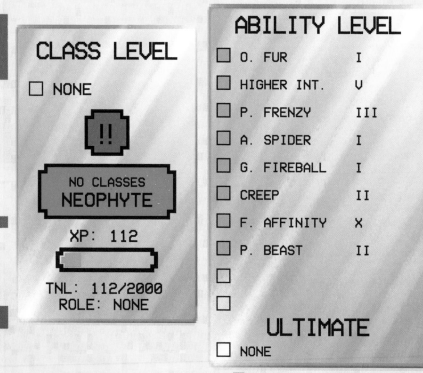

CLASS LEVEL

☐ NONE

!!

NO CLASSES
NEOPHYTE

XP: 112

TNL: 112/2000
ROLE: NONE

ABILITY LEVEL

☐	O. FUR	I
☐	HIGHER INT.	V
☐	P. FRENZY	III
☐	A. SPIDER	I
☐	G. FIREBALL	I
☐	CREEP	II
☐	F. AFFINITY	X
☐	P. BEAST	II
☐		
☐		

ULTIMATE
☐ NONE

I didn't have a class.

So I was a **Neophyte,** which was a nice way to say . . . I was a noob.

By gaining a class, you gain bonuses, as well as access to certain abilities. A **Wizard** could learn spells, while a **Warrior** might learn some kind of shield move. I had 112 **experience points,** or XP, which is a rather pitiful amount.

"What's **TNL?**" I asked.

"**To next level.** It means how much XP you need to . . . um . . . reach the next level."

I pointed to the text at the very bottom. "And **role?**"

"Oh, that. Depending on what class you end up choosing, your role will be **defensive, offensive, or supportive.** Someone with a supportive role is called a '**support.**' They specialize in abilities that assist their allies. Someone with a defensive role is a '**tank.**' They're usually on the front line, as they're harder to take down. Finally, those with offensive roles are—"

"**All about damage.**"

"Yep. See, you're catching on."

I winked. "Well, I **do** have ten **INT.**"

But I was just putting on a show. After everything that had happened today, my head was starting to hurt. In a single day, I'd learned:

33

1.) Runt and Breeze were not currently in the village.

2.) **Terrarians** were all quite different—from skin color to personality and hairstyle.

3.) The **continent** we were living on was very big.

4.) Every creature had these things called "**attributes**."

5.) I was literally a **Neophyte**.

This morning, I went to the dining hall.

I was looking for a **decent breakfast,** you know? Then a young man waved at me.

His name was **Kaeleb,** and he was eating . . . well, I'm not so sure that what he was eating could be called "**food.**"

Oh, it looked kind of like a vegetable, sure. Like a huge turnip, really. But the scent it gave off was **nauseating.** It turned my stomach.

What should I have for breakfast? Oh, let's see—anything **but** that.

I backed up at once. "What **is** that thing?"

"A **boag.** Want one?"

I gave him a look. How could someone eat such a thing?! Then my eyes started watering. The fumes that thing gave off! Even the stuff I smelled in the Nether wasn't that bad!

"Back in our world," Kae said, "we had onions and garlic. A boag is the closest thing we've found in Aetheria." He took another bite. "An acquired taste, I must admit. Although I've read they're quite healthy. They'll also grow anywhere. It's a staple food of mountaineers and hermits."

All right, so I was still as curious as I've always been—the Nether still hadn't taken that away from me. I did end up trying one . . . and I spat it out right away. If I had to describe the taste of a boag with just one word, that word would be "assault."

"That's all right," Kae said. "As I said, it's an acquired taste." He held up another vegetable. This one was deep reddish-brown with golden orange leaves.

"This is an autug. They're even more resilient than boags, but they don't taste as good. Also takes some effort to bite into."

He gave me the vegetable, and I stashed it in my inventory. No way was I going to try it. It was hard as stone and had a metallic scent. "Where'd you get these things, anyway? I've never heard of them."

"Yeah. Not surprising. They're native to other realms. A trader came by with a few of them, and I thought they could come in handy later.

If **Villagetown** ever fell and we had to live somewhere cold, we'd at least be able to grow food."

I took another bite and winced.
"Let's hope it <u>never comes to that</u>."

I ran into Leo and Lylla as I was leaving the dining hall.

After yet another "**haiwoo**," Leo glanced inside the hall, to the far corner, as did Lylla. A single person was there. **A young man I didn't know.**

"Great," Lylla said. "He's back in time for the meeting."

Leo kept staring at him, his fists shaking slightly. "Can't believe **that jerk** got promoted!"

"Who is he?" I asked.

"**Ched. The Legion's top scout.** Well, tied with Kae."

As Leo said this, Cobalt and Rubinia, having ordered food at the counter, went over to Ched and sat down beside him.

"He's got his own little crew within **the Legion**," Lylla said. "Anyway, Ched might be good with a bow, but **he's not a good person.** He shouldn't even be part of this clan. **Stay away from him, Eeebs.**"

"Okay."

Again, no arguments there. I'd seen him a couple times already, and he always looked grumpy.

Ched finished his meal, said goodbye to his friends, and made his way to the entrance, walking past us. That's when I noticed his shirt.

(His shirt apparently read: "I H8" followed by . . . a zombie face?)

"Why aren't you in clan uniform?" Leo asked him.

"I just got back after being outside for two whole days," he said. "I was **crit** by a **skeleton's arrow, then I got jumped by an owltroll, and while I was trying to heal up from all that, a small army of cake slimes found me.** So do you really think I care about clan uniforms right now? I just wanna relax."

"Yeah, well, you—"

"Leave me alone, noober." He walked away.

"'I hate zombies' was written on his shirt," I said after he left. "What does that mean, 'I hate zombies'? Why?"

"Actually, the face on his shirt represents **monsters**," Lylla said. "He has this thing against them. It's a long story, and I don't really feel like talking about him."

"Same here," Leo said.

And today I learned that the Legion has their own version of the angry man with the eyebrows!

So Ched really hates monsters, huh? I'm guessing by the look on his face that I'm included in that category.

Oh no! I forgot to ask!
What's an owltroll?!

Going clockwise from Kolbert,
in the lower left: Ched, Becca, Krafty, Amber,
Cobalt, Rubinia, Zain, Ghost, Steph, Lylla,
Leonardios, Kae, BlastLight. Kolbert and Hurion
were facing everyone. I was next to Kae, but
there's no way I'm going to draw myself sitting
at a table. I'm trying to repress the memory.

Steph came into my room and told me there was a clan meeting, then she dragged me off.

I'm not even part of the **Lost Legion,** so I couldn't understand why I had to attend. And I had to sit at a table! A table! **In a chair!**

As a former animal, I'm not too fond of tables and chairs. Especially chairs. I mean, if they were made of something soft, like wool, well, I could get used to them. It would be easy. But chairs were always made of wood. Always. Why? **It's like sitting on a rock.**

41

I've been trying really hard to understand these strange people, but **I swear . . .**

That night's meeting was about several topics.

I'll share each one in order, with its own update.

Of course, the very first thing they discussed was **the Prophecy** and the **mysterious blue "thing" named Eeebs.**

Steph had brought a ton of food. The light brown things were **cocoa bean rolls.** Even though I'm a cat, I thought they were **magnificent.**

But there was another food item that was **several tiers of deliciousness** above even that. **Cinnamuffins.**

They were enchanted food of the highest caliber.

I'd even say that **cinnamuffins** were, quite simply, the best thing I'd **ever** eaten. I can't even begin to describe the taste. And each one increased each of my attributes by twenty-five (for one hour).

Normally, you'd need at least 750 Crafting skill and this thing called an **"Aeon Forge"** to craft a cinnamuffin. But a Baker can bypass that with the **Makeshift Muffin** ability.

What does all of that mean? **Don't know and don't care.** As long as I get to eat more of them.

"The very first thing we'll discuss during tonight's meeting," Kolbert said as he took a bite of his cinnamuffin. He paused. "Wow. Um, the first thing we'll discuss is how **amazing these things are.**"

"Yeah, that ability is almost unfair," Kae said. "Honestly, just because of that Muffin ability, the Bakers are almost OP."

Steph smiled at me. "Well? What do you think, Eeebs?"

I stared down at the table where my muffin had been, wishing I had another. "I think fish is no longer my <u>favorite</u> food."

There isn't much I can add here that I haven't already gone over.

To recap, **the Prophecy is a quest designed by the Immortal named Entity.**

I'm not the only one involved. Far from it. If this quest were a massive tree, then I'd just be one branch. Most of **the Legionnaires** would be even smaller branches. And that sword of Kolbert's would be the largest branch of all, if not the trunk itself.

Kolbert held the sword out before everyone.

"Don't think of this weapon as mine," he said. "Entity merely entrusted me with its safekeeping. In truth, it's ours. I've spoken with Breeze's father, who seems to know the past well. He believes that it's not just a sword. That it's more of a key. Once reforged, it will help us in many ways. Of all our current goals, restoring this weapon is the most important and the most long-term one. It's our **endgame.**"

From what I understood, once that sword was repaired, the enchantments it contained would be strong enough to help us defeat the **evil wizard** trying to take over the world.

The Eyeless One.

Otherwise known as Ol' NoPupils.

Otherwise known as The Unseeing One.

Otherwise known as He Who Never Blinks or The Forever Eternal.
Or He Who Wears No Underpants. Ghost referred to him as that
earlier. What underpants are, I didn't know. But there's one thing I
did know:

I was so done
with these names.

Kae had been eating those horrible vegetables for the past week.

Well, an hour ago, just before the meeting, he'd consumed his **fiftieth boag.** So his vitality (VIT) immediately increased by one point.

As disgusting as those things were, eating enough of them would permanently increase your **VIT** a little, giving a small boost in health, resistance to poison, and so on.

"We're talking about **free stats,**" Kolbert said. "I want each of you eating at least one per day."

You can guess how that went over. Lots of groans and a great many sighs.

Well, except for Kae. "C'mon, guys. If you think about it, it's almost like our duty to eat them. I mean, if doing so increases your chances of survival by even 1%, why not?"

"Yeah, well, do you think there might be a way to make them more . . . palatable?" Zain asked.

Steph threw a large book down on the table and began flipping through it. "I think I saw a lasagna recipe in here," she said. "Ah. Here it is. And yeah. **Boags are one of the alternative ingredients.**"

Leo looked at Steph doubtfully. "**Boag lasagna?** Would we still get stat increases from that?"

"There's only one way to find out," Kolbert said. "Who's willing to become the Legion's first official **guinea pig?**"

Only Kae and Ghost raised their hands. Although Ghost hated the taste of boags as much as anyone else, he was a so-called **power gamer,** meaning he was all about the stats.

"Craft away," he said to Steph. "And give me a full stack. In fact, **forget lasagna, or even eating them raw.** If you say they give **free stats,** let's see whether we can make juice out of those things."

Becca and Cobalt gave him a disgusted look.

As for me, well, when Kolbert asked whether there was anyone else who wanted to begin eating boags "**in the name of science,**" I sank lower in my seat.

I bet only my ears were visible.
Until I lowered **them, too.**

The meeting's next topic involved pretty much the coolest thing I'd ever seen.

I was well aware that magic existed in the world. I was also aware that some people were capable of casting spells. Yet I was **not** aware of just how amazinf the more powerful spells could be. *(Genuine typo there. I'm leaving it, though, as it captures my excitement.)*

Standing before everyone, Hurion took a **brilliant white coin** from his belt pouch and held it before us. **It glimmered in the light.**

"We need to decide what to do with this," he said, stepping forward so I could get a better look. "This is a **wish token. I won it by accomplishing a major quest in the capital.**"

"Some items out there contain spells," Kolbert said. "For example, a staff might hold a **healing spell.** By invoking it, you could essentially cast the spell. But many of these items have charges, meaning they can be used only a limited number of times."

"And a wish token has exactly one charge," Hurion said. "It's a spell by the same name. **Wish.** It's an ultimate ability. The strongest known."

"An **ultimate** is pretty much just a really powerful ability," Lylla added. "There are hundreds of them. Some provide **massive healing or protection;** others create **huge explosions.**"

"**Wish,** though . . ." Leo stared at the coin dreamily. "That spell is in a tier of its own." He sighed. "You're so lucky, Hurion."

"Well, what are some of the possible choices?" I asked.

"Let's just show him," Becca said. "That'll save a lot of time. Besides, the spell effect **is** pretty cool."

"Yeah, Hurion's actually used that token to cast Wish several times already," Leo said. "This weird girl appears with a list of options. One of the options is **Cancel, which ends the spell without any effect and doesn't consume the wish.**"

"Oh." I was **way** out of my league, here.

I'd seen only the most **basic abilities,** like my breath, and had no idea what Leo meant by **"options."**

Kolbert looked at me understandingly, then nodded at Hurion, as if to say, **"Please show this nooby kitten how cool higher-level magic can be."**

Hurion stepped back, holding the token before him, and closed his eyes. A second or two later, a **gust of wind swirled** through the room, and the **torches dimmed.** There was a loud and deep sound, like a **creeper** exploding in the distance. It was so loud I felt the room shaking beneath me, and the flasks of coffee began rattling and slowly dancing across the table.

Then, in a **flash of white light,** a most **unusual-looking girl** appeared.

Not only was she hovering in the air but also she had **greenish hair and skin** and a **pair of gossamer wings. Tiny iridescent motes fell around her like dust.** She held out a screen of ghostly blue light.

WHAT IS YOUR WISH?
SPELL BARRIER
BANISH MONSTERS
FORCEFIELD
BLESSING OF KINGS
DIVINE INTERVENTION
SUMMON EMERALDS
REQUEST ASSISTANCE
TRANSFER PARTY
SPEAK WITH IMMORTAL
WEAKEN ONE MONSTER
CALL A FLYING MOUNT
BOOST SKILLS OF PARTY
CAST ANY TWO ULTIMATES
UNLOCK ANY DOOR
MODIFY CURRENT BIOME
OPEN PORTAL TO ANOTHER REALM
ENCHANT AN ITEM
WIZINVIS
CREATE ANY ONE ITEM
CANCEL

Indeed, Wish seemed to be capable of **almost anything.**

Some of the options I saw were pretty self-explanatory.
Others, not so much. I assumed the Legionnaires knew what each option did.

As everyone stared at the **elflike girl,** irritation flashed across her face. "I hope you've finally decided what you're going to wish for," she said to Hurion. **"This is the fifth time you've summoned me this week!"**

"Sorry," Hurion said. "I still haven't made up my mind. **Cancel.**"

She glared at him. **"Again?"**

"Cancel **is** an available option," he said. "I've decided to save my wish for later."

"Hmmph! This is the last time!" The screen burst into **glimmering motes,** then the **bizarre-looking girl** flew over to Hurion and poked him in the shoulder. "Next time you call me, you better use that wish of yours for something, or **I'm taking it away! Got it?!"**

With that, she **vanished in a flash of light.** The torches grew brighter again.

"And that was . . . ?" This was all I could articulate.

Leo shrugged. "No idea. We've tried talking to her before, but every time, she just vanishes. She looks like a **limoniad,** but those wings are **faerie-like.**"

51

I assumed those were other races, but who cares? I'd just witnessed the most **powerful spell ever known.** It had its limitations, and you had to choose something on that list, but, still, **how amazing was that?**

BlastLight seemed to know as little as I did. "What does each option do, exactly?"

Kae pulled a **golden book** from his bag and set it on the table. "It's all in here." *(The book's title was Advanced Wizardry VIII: On Wishes.)*

BlastLight **jumped up** from his seat and came to sit next to me, and we skimmed through it together. **Spell Barrier** could make an entire party all but immune to magic. **Forcefield** was similar but for physical attacks. **Blessing of Kings** could give Strength VII and Regeneration VII to a "small army"—up to sixty people. **Modify Current Biome** allowed you to enchant an entire biome. **Wizinvis** was the highest form of invisibility, rendering even your armor and other items invisible. **Request Assistance** summoned a "greater being" that would fight for you. (Sadly, **Summon Emeralds** had a limit of 10,000.)

"At any rate, we've been discussing the **Wish problem** for weeks," Kolbert said. "We've narrowed it down to two options. One option would be to **use the wish to modify or enchant this biome.** The best enchantment possible, given our situation, is probably the **Sacred enchantment.** With that in place, **undead and anything with**

52

an affinity to evil would take damage over time, like how a zombie burns in sunlight. This enchantment would **last forever, or until dispelled.** And even though the effect wouldn't be very noticeable right away, it would help Villagetown for a long time."

"And the other option?" Zain asked before I had the chance.

Kolbert's expression grew a little darker. "Well, Eeebs claims a dragon will attack Villagetown in the future. The **Eyeless One** himself said that he would send more monsters. **We could save Hurion's wish, keep it as a sort of panic button.** If Villagetown ever faced an attack we couldn't possibly handle, we could then request assistance."

"Whatever we summoned would be **unimaginably strong,**" Hurion said. "At least level 200. And probably **something huge,** with a strong **Breath weapon** or wide area attacks. It would take out every monster in sight, sure. Yet it could take part of Villagetown with it. . . ."

"My vote is for **enchanting the biome,**" Leo said. "I mean, **summoning a huge monster just sounds dangerous.**"

Ched sighed. "Do you remember how many zombies we faced last time? **We barely pulled through.** I'm voting for the beast."

"But we gotta think of the baby villagers," Leo said.

"Whatever. You're practically a **baby villager** yourself, with that **Combat skill** of yours."

Glaring at Ched, Leo shot up from his seat. "It's level 95 now, idiot!"

Ched shrugged. "So what? Even those villager kids have hit a hundred by now. In fact, I'm willing to bet fishing's the only thing you beat them at. Yeah, I heard about how you always come back with stacks of fish every time you go 'scouting.'"

"You seem to hear about a lot of things," Leo replied. At this point, he'd walked around the table and was standing before Ched. "Is that why people call you 'Grapevine'?"

At this, Ched became so angry he almost looked like Drill. He jumped up, glaring at Leo. "At least no one's calling me a noob, noob!"

"Yeah?!" Leo shoved him. "You wanna duel?!"

Ched shoved back. "Show me what you've got, Neophyte!"

They shoved each other again, and almost everyone else got up. Some went to Ched's side, the others to Leo's. Someone pushed me off my seat (although I was thankful for that).

Then everyone began shouting at once as Leo and Ched grappled with one another.

"I'll smash you, noob!"

"Not if I crit you first, noob!"

"Enough!" Kolbert pushed his way between them. "We've been at each other's throats for far too long. It has to stop. Now. If anyone wants to duel with a fellow clan member, they'll have to duel with me first."

"Whatever." Ched stormed off, muttering as he pushed through the crowd.

"What a bunch of noobery . . ." Cobalt followed him, along with Becca and Rubinia.

Then Leo took off with Kae and Ghost.

The rest quickly shuffled out of the room, until it was just me and Kolbert, who gave me a **weary smile.** "Welcome to the Legion."

Yeahhh. I hadn't been hanging out with these people for very long, but they clearly had problems working together.

It must have been hard for them, I guess, adjusting to this new world. **It had been hard for me, too.**

As I'm writing these words, I'm in bed, under the covers.

I know that's normal for most people, but for me . . . well, it was all I could do not to curl up on the carpet.

That morning, I tried using the **tellstone** again. I thought maybe I could see how Breeze was doing.

At first, the crystal's surface only revealed some wavy orange lines and a sharp noise, like **hissing or crackling.** Then the following appeared . . .

They were in some **dark place,** like a cave.

Although their weapons were drawn, they weren't fighting. Actually, they seemed somewhat calm, looking around.

"We need to hurry," I heard Breeze say. "Things are getting pretty crazy back home."

"They'll calm down once we return with that forge," Runt said. "Um, should I use my shield now?"

I tried speaking to them. 'Hey! Breeze! Can you hear me?'

She couldn't. Then the image cut out.

Nothing happened when I tried viewing them again, just more crackling.

Seriously, what was up with this crystal thing? It barely worked. Someone needed to work on their Crafting skill.

Oh well, wherever those two were, they seemed to be doing okay.

I just hope they come back soon.

While exploring the courtyard, **I ran into Cobalt.**

I didn't know what to say to him. He was close friends with Ched, so I figured he might have been just as **ill-tempered.**

He wasn't, though.

"Sorry about yesterday, Eeebs. Ched can get a little intense at times."

"What happened back there? Why were Leo and Ched 'at each other's throats,' as Kolbert put it?"

"Ched is part of a small but **vocal group of Legionnaires** who've been pushing for all of us to head out more. They think every Legionnaire should start **leveling up** as much as possible. Even though it's risky, they feel **we won't survive** unless we become stronger. Then there are those who want to **play it safe.** They believe **we should stay in Villagetown** until we really understand how this world works. **Leo's one of the most vocal members** of that group. As for the rest, they're just trying to get by."

"Why is he like that? Ched, I mean."

"He's seen a lot since **the Cataclysm.** Soon after we woke up here, we were attacked, and a friend of ours was . . ."

"You mean, he died?"

"Guess so. We figured he might've **respawned, but we never saw him again.** His name was **Aram.**"

"What happened?"

"We were still on the beach," Cobalt said. "A lot of us woke up there, nineteen of us. **And, man, everyone was just losing it. I mean total chaos.** And even as the sun started to set, people just kept panicking. We had no materials and no torches, and soon after it got dark, the undead just swarmed from the forest to the shore. It all happened so fast, and . . . before anyone knew it, **Aram was gone.** Just gone." He shuddered. "The next day, Ched became one of the first Legionnaires to try '**playing the game.**' He helped build the first shelter and crafted the first weapons. If you ask around, many will tell you he's **too hotheaded.** Still, he's always been there for us. **Aram was his best friend,** and he vowed to never let anything like that happen to anyone else."

And that was Ched's story.

Cobalt said everyone among the Legion has their own story, and after hearing Ched's, **I was determined to record them.**

There was yet another incident, **almost like a riot.**

Most of the Legionnaires—**the lower ranks**—had rooms in the basement of the keep. There were at least fifty rooms down there. Yet roughly half the boys had rooms that were just two blocks by one block.

"My room is literally a bed," Leo said. "That's it. Just a bed."

"Mine too," Ghost said. "And you know what's funny? Not one of the girls has a room as small as ours. **And our hallways are so narrow!** In the morning, you can barely squeeze past all the people."

Of course, I'd explored the lower floor myself, and the boys had a point.

"Becca's the worst," Ghost said. "Not only does she have the biggest room among lower-ranked Legionnaires but also she has an enchanted bed and one of those mini-chests to save space! That mini-chest was once part of the **clan loot!** We never even voted on who got to keep it!"

Leo crossed his arms. "She shouldn't be given extra stuff just because she's a girl."

BOYS'
HALL

GIRLS'
HALL

"Well, before we even decided on building, we all agreed that the girls would get more space," Kolbert said. "Living here has been particularly hard for them."

At least ten Legionnaires surrounded Kolbert, shouting angrily:
"But it's been hard on us, too!"

"I'm about to quit this noob clan!"

"I don't even have space for an item chest!"

Chivalry is one of our codes of honor," Hurion calmly told them.

But I could tell Kolbert was struggling to keep his cool. "Fine. Someone can have my room. I don't care."

I backed up slowly. No way was I getting involved.

It's official. The Legion has serious problems. Still, who could blame them for being angry? If I had to sleep in a room like Leo's, I'd be pretty upset, too.

Compare his room to Becca's.

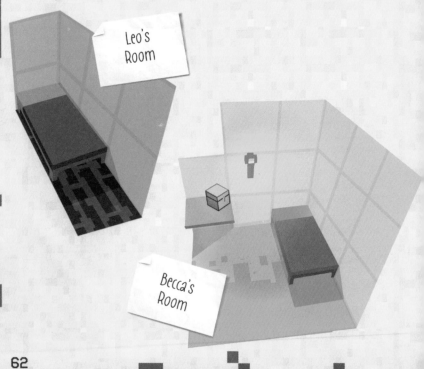

Leo's Room

Becca's Room

That afternoon, **Steph burst** into my room. Followed by Lylla. Then Amber, Becca, Rubinia, and BlastLight.

They were followed by a villager named **Puddles.** I had no idea who he was, but the way he smiled creeped me out. "Why, yes," he said. "I can see potential here."

Still on my bed, I backed up against the wall. "Potential for **what?!**"

"Since you are linked to **the Prophecy,**" Lylla replied, "the **Eyeless One sees you as a threat.** That means you need to learn how to blend in. Villagetown is relatively safe, but what if you have to go to the capital someday? Pretty hard to be **inconspicuous as a blue ocelot.**"

"We only want you to try on some clothes," Steph said.

"That's it?"

"That's it."

Okay, so I wasn't **exactly thrilled** with the idea. But I'd already learned how to walk like they do, and I'd already used some tools like **fishing rods.** Why stop there? If these people had told me that **strapping big blocks** of cheese to my feet was completely normal, not only would I have believed them but also I'd have at least tried. **I had to understand their culture.** Greyfellow had told me to learn as much as I could, and **I wasn't going to let him down.**

So I followed them up to the surface. It was nice getting some fresh air. And we went to the **Clothing Castle,** where I ended up doing more than trying on a new outfit. . . .

First, they had me drink a **Wildshape potion.** When consumed by an animal, it turns said animal into its "anthropomorphic version"—**more like a human.** It wasn't that bad. My limbs grew a bit longer, which made standing and walking upright easier. **But that was about it.**

I cringed when I learned that this physical effect was **permanent until dispelled.** I cringed even further when I learned that this was only the first step.

The second step involved a **"maquillage."** You know how a crafting table has these little saws and hammers and stuff on it? Well, a maquillage was just like that. Only it had an assortment of combs, brushes, and scissors. This kind of block was used for "skin alteration," which doesn't refer to one's actual skin, but one's appearance.

Basically, they modified my skin. When I saw myself in this thing called a **"mirror,"** I almost cried.

They dyed my fur a shade of blue. There's a race of cat people who have this color of fur. They're called **shadowpaws.** If I stood on my hind legs while wearing clothes, I could pass as one of them. **Well, almost.**

But this **so-called skin alteration** didn't stop there, oh no. They also puffed up the fur on top of my head and dyed it darker blue to look like human hair, **because that's what that race of humanoid cats apparently does.**

They also gave me a weapon: a thin sword called a **rapier.** When I wielded it, everyone but Puddles laughed. Why?! What's so funny about me wielding a sword?!

I've gotta tell you that drawing the following picture was probably the **hardest thing** I've ever done.

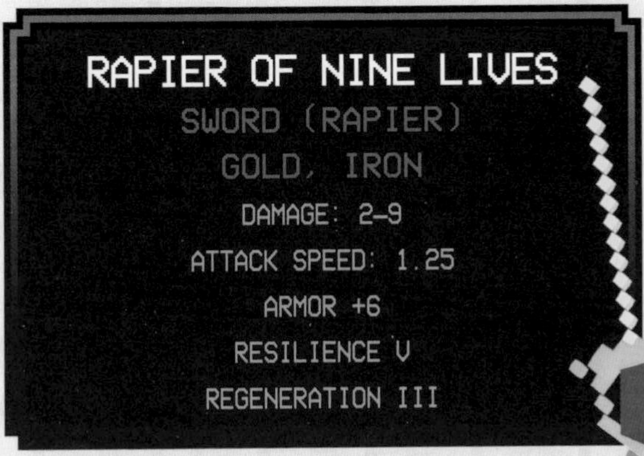

RAPIER OF NINE LIVES
SWORD (RAPIER)
GOLD, IRON
DAMAGE: 2-9
ATTACK SPEED: 1.25
ARMOR +6
RESILIENCE V
REGENERATION III

BlastLight said I looked "**soooo fancy.**"

Personally, I found it odd to be given a sword with not only **Armor** but also **Resilience** and **Regeneration.** What kind of noob do they take me for? Those are defensive enchantments!

65

Puddles clapped his hands. "Dare I say you could pass for a prince! Among the cat people, I mean!"

Circling me, Lylla nodded in approval. "All you need to do now is get better at walking, and you won't draw so much attention. You can just tell people you're from **Bramblecleft.** That's the main city of the cat people. It's in another dimension; they come to the **Overworld** to trade every now and then. Oh, and you can dispel the effect of **Wildshape** whenever you like. We have a lot of those potions."

"That's nice, but . . ." I gave my rapier a disapproving look. "**You guys don't actually expect me to learn how to use this, do you?**" I gestured to my gear. "Or . . . **fight in this stuff?**"

"Actually, it might be a good idea," Becca said. "Otherwise, you'd be holding yourself back."

"Why? Oh. Wait. I know." As I remembered what Kolbert said about items several days ago, my ears became as flat as my voice. "**Because enchantments.**"

"Pretty much," Becca said. "Your **claw attacks** will get stronger as you level up, and so will your **natural armor, but you're not even level 1,** so you'll be much more effective with some gear. Learn to use a sword and thank us later, K?"

"**. . . Oookay.**"

Emphasis on the *O* there, a slightly long sound, followed by a weaker *kay*, which should have made clear my uncertainty right then and there, slash confusion, slash cluelessness, slash I just wanted to eat cinnamuffins, **oookay?**

The thought of going outside dressed like this made me shudder.

You know that kid who helped me build the chicken house? He was known as the **village noob.** Everyone was always laughing at the silly things he did. But I'd be replacing him soon. As soon as I left the **Clothing Castle.**

Actually, my new appearance might make people scream. Especially the villager kids. Imagine a big thing walking around just like a human or a villager, **only it's got whiskers, a tail, and light-blue fur**—and the fur on top of its head is puffed out like a **baby bird's feathers** when it's cold. And half the village already thought I was a monster. So . . .

Then I thought about home. My friends back in the Nether. My mom. Mom must be so worried about me, I thought. And everyone in **Lavacrest** must be facing monsters by now. And here I'm fretting over my appearance, what others might think of me. How sad is that?

I stood up straighter. **Yeah? Who cares if I look silly?** If wearing boots increases my chances of being able to help them by even 0.001%, fine—I'll wear boots. I'll even throw on a helmet made out of a giant potato if that's what it takes. And if eating enough of those disgusting vegetables Kae likes to eat really does increase my vitality, well, **I will eat those vegetables, mashed or boiled and sautéed in dirt. I don't care!**

Nodding to myself, I checked out my gear.

This stuff had once belonged to Kolbert. It was part of this group of items known as the "**Neophyte set.**" Every Terrarian arrived in this world wearing stuff like this.

Yep. I'm literally wearing **hand-me-down noob gear.**

Normally, such items have no stats to speak of. But Rubinia threw some enchantments on everything to help me out. She's an **Enchanter,** so that was pretty much her only job within the Legion.

NEOPHYTE'S BLAZER OF NEOPHYTIAN PROTECTION
CLOTHING (TORSO) –
WOOL, COPPER
+3 ARMOR – RESILIENCE V
POISON RESISTANCE II

PROTECTION OF THE CLUELESS: CRITICAL HITS FROM ANY OPPONENT AT LEAST FIVE LEVELS ABOVE YOU ARE REDUCED BY 50%.

BEGINNER PANTALOONS OF NOOBIC FURY
CLOTHING (LEGS) – WOOL
+3 ARMOR – RESILIENCE V – POISON RESISTANCE II

NOOBIC FURY: WHENEVER YOU ATTACK AN OPPONENT WHO IS AT LEAST FIVE LEVELS ABOVE YOU, YOU HAVE A 10% CHANCE OF ATTACKING TWO ADDITIONAL TIMES.

NOVITIATE'S GOBLINKICKERS
OF HEROIC RETREAT
CLOTHING (FEET) — WOOL, COPPER

+2 ARMOR

GOBLIN SLAYER: YOUR STR IS INCREASED BY 15 WHEN YOU FIGHT
KOBOLDS AND OTHER GOBLINKIND.
HEROIC RETREAT: WHILE MOVING AWAY FROM NEARBY ENEMIES, YOU
GAIN A 10% BONUS TO MOVEMENT SPEED.

Yep. **More Resilience.** That provided **protection against crits. Protection of the Clueless** provided additional protection against crits from enemies at least five levels higher than me. *(Since I was a Neophyte, that meant pretty much everything outside basic zombies and slimes.)* Finally, two items had **Poison Resistance.**

I found that enchantment a **little unsettling.**

Call me crazy, but there was just something weird about this abundance of defensive enchantments. Like the Legion was **really** interested in keeping me alive. **Why this spell specifically?** Were they expecting me to get jumped by cave spiders or something?

When I asked about this, Puddles laughed nervously. "Oh, don't **worry! It's just a precaution!**"

These boots raised another question. **Did goblins actually exist?** Judging by the enchantment they carried, they did. Huh. I'd always thought they were only imaginary. They were in several ocelot bedtime stories.

"**Goblinkickers,** huh?" I kicked the air. "I've heard of goblins before, but **what's a kobold?**"

"They're like goblins," Lylla said, "only a bit smaller. They're pretty good at Crafting, too. They know how to make **advanced siege weaponry.** Although we have yet to see any of them—**kobolds,** I mean. Ched claims to have encountered some goblins on his last trek out. So we thought the **Goblin Slayer** enchantment might be useful."

"Oh. How about we change the subject. Can we go now?"

Lylla laughed. "Wow, you think we're done?"

"Kinda?"

"Wrong. You'll need a **scabbard.** Oh, and maybe a belt."

At this, Puddles spun around quickly. It was one of the **weirdest things** I'd seen so far. And I'd seen a lot. For example, Ched throwing an **enderpotato** across the dining hall in anger because I'd been snooping around in his room while he was gone.

"I'm glad you reminded me, Lylla!" Puddles shouted. *(It was weird to hear someone shout when they weren't angry.)* "I almost forgot! **It's time to do a little trading!** I mean **shopping!** Oh, I almost feel like a Terrarian, hanging out with you folks!"

Just as I was thinking how weird Puddles sounded, Leo zoomed into the Clothing Castle. "**Haiwoo!!**"

Amber returned his greeting with a greeting that was **equally bizarre.** "Holo, Leo."

BlastLight, too. "Holwoo."

Seriously? How many different ways were there to say hello, anyway? I waved at him. "Um, holwoopineapple?" **Okay, so I just made that up.** I had no idea whether it was actually a proper Earth greeting.

Thankfully, Leo somehow seemed to understand this. "Hey, Eeebs." Then he seemed to really notice me. "Oh. Um. Wow. Nice . . . gear."

"Thanks?"

He smiled. "Well, keep it up. I'd love to chat, but I gotta go. I'm already late for **wall duty!** Oh, and someone please show Eeebs how to **wield** that rapier properly, huh? **Baiwoo!**"

(Whether villager or Terrarian, people like Drill, Puddles, and Leo are so zany, so prone to random outbursts of pure emotion, they make the monsters of Lavacrest look like an army of zombies at a backward door convention. That is to say, boring.)

We went to Villagetown's **Finest Arms,** where Puddles traded with this old villager guy, **Leaf.** In the end, I was handed a "scabbard"—for my sword—then a belt and belt pouch. The latter is what people use for additional item storage.

Then we went to the village hall. It had a huge dining hall, and the mayor ate there often. The hall was empty, though, besides us. The mayor was inspecting some **defensive measures** the villagers had come up with, including "trapdoor pits"—whatever those were. What is important here is that I spent the next hour sitting at a table. In a chair. Learning about such things as plates and flasks and dinner courses and table manners and, and . . . I need to stop writing about this now.

I'll come back and write about good stuff after I have another cinnamuffin.

An hour or so after dinner, we were all standing outside the village hall.

It was **dark and a bit windy** and chilly out. Puddles had already left to go speak with the mayor, and Lylla and the rest were about to head back to the keep. I told them to go on without me. I just wanted to walk around, get some more **fresh air.**

Steph was the last to leave. She gestured toward a **huge stone building** across from the hall. Unlike the hall, there wasn't anything fancy about its construction. It was just a **monolithic mass** of cobblestone obscuring part of the star-filled sky.

"That's the **opera house,**" she said. "The villagers have been working on it whenever they get a chance. The mayor thought it would be a **good idea.** Entertain everyone, distract them from their worries, you know?"

"What's an opera house for?"

"**To watch operas and plays.** I'll be performing there in two days, along with Leo, Amber, and a few others. We'll be doing a **reenactment** of how we arrived in Aetheria. This'll help the villagers understand us better." Steph was smiling. "You should come. You'll learn more about us, too."

"I'll be there," I said. "**Just don't expect me to be able to clap with these paws.**"

Steph nodded. "Well, I'm going back to the keep. See ya there?"

"See ya."

That's another way of saying goodbye. The other girls all used it before they left. I'm learning so much.

After she left, I walked calmly down the streets, scanning the rose bushes, the **white quartz columns,** the **fluttering banners,** and the **lines of oak blocks** that once held cake. Maybe I was hoping a monster would jump out and attack me. Everyone in the Legion was level 7, and for me, level 1 seemed so far away. . . .

I only saw a few villagers **scurrying** home, and no one I recognized. However, soon after I turned a corner, I heard a voice to my left.

"Good evening."

It was a woman. I could barely see her. She was standing in a **dark corner** of an alcove along the hall's east side.

Strangely, I caught a whiff of flowers. Because of my **refined** sense of smell and my **former pastime** of bounding through woods, I could identify most flowers by their scent. Yet I couldn't recognize this one. I got the feeling that this woman was a long way from home.

"It's a nice evening, don't you think?" she said, with the hint of a smile.

Given how cold it'd become, I couldn't agree. To say nothing of what had happened earlier. "It's a **bit nippy,** actually."

"I was referring to the stars," she said. "The sky is clear tonight."

She drew closer. In the light, I could see that her skin was **unusually pale,** and her ears came to a point. I'd seen only one other person like her, and that was a very long time ago, near my home—my old home, **deep in the forest** to the west.

She also wore a **violet crystal pendant** shaped like a moon. **It glowed faintly.**

"The monsters have been growing stronger as of late," she continued, looking past me to the sky. "And this coincides with the return of the **Crying Star.**"

"The Crying Star?"

I turned around as she drew closer, pointing to a spot in the sky. This close, the floral scent was nearly overwhelming.

"There."

There must have been thousands of stars in the night sky, each **glimmering green, blue, or violet.** And there was the **green**

Milky Way stretching across it all. Back when I was still a kitten, I'd spent so many nights with my friends looking up at them, lying in the grass, wondering what they were. Yet I don't remember ever having seen the star she pointed to. I would've remembered that **smoldering red speck.**

"In the coming months, it will become more pronounced," she said. "Large enough to be mistaken for a second moon. But if you look more closely, you'll see that it is more like a group of red stars packed tightly together, like the **fragments of a broken crystal.**"

"What is it, exactly?"

"There is one **magister** who claims it is a single star that was shattered long ago and that its smaller fragments, many shaped like tears, are orbiting a much larger mass. I don't know whether it is possible for a star like that to exist, yet . . . everything he has foretold so far has come to pass. Perhaps this is why I stand before you now."

"Wait, you've been . . . looking for me?"

"Only to make sure that you are well. **I'm afraid we have different paths.**"

"I don't understand."

"There are few who do. What I can tell you is . . . **when the Crying Star has risen completely, so that its hue can be seen across the plains, all of Aetheria will be put to the test.**"

"How long until that happens?"

"All signs suggest **no sooner than three waves of the silver moon.**"

Three waves of the . . . oh. Well, that's a weird way of putting it. Couldn't she have just said "roughly three months from now"?

"Forgive me for being so direct," I said, "but . . . do you have **any advice** for me? Anything specific?"

"Yes. You are needed here. Follow the fire."

Before I could ask anything else, **she darted off** into the darkness, her footsteps light and her cloak rustling.

I spent the next minute just standing there, thinking about what she'd said. **"Follow the fire"?** What does that mean? I laughed a little and shook my head, then I took off running through the streets. *And that's why I love Villagetown,* I thought, zooming past the houses— it was the first time I'd ever run on two legs. *There's always something* <u>crazy</u> *going on around here.*

When I got back to the keep, I ran into Kolbert and told him about my **encounter.**

He didn't know what to think of it, either. Apparently, he was as curious as I was, and he asked Kae to try tracking her, as in the ability **Track.** Tracking let him see the traces left by anything that walked, crawled, or otherwise moved along the ground. Most tracks couldn't be seen without this ability.

Kae did manage to follow her. But when he finally caught up to her, he only had time to see her climb onto a **large gray wolf** and ride off.

The Legionnaires thought she was a **moon elf. They often used wolves as mounts, and their skin color ranged from dark gray to an almost pure white like hers.** Oddly, moon elves were almost never seen outside **Ravensong,** the forest to the northwest. What was a moon elf scout doing so far from home? It's a **mystery.**

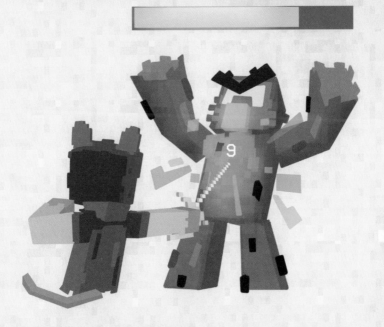

I practiced all day against an **owltroll.**

In truth, it was just a copy of one. **A training golem.** Besides being made of **enchanted wood**, it was like an owltroll in every way. It had a **big beak** and a **single huge eye.** It even displayed an owltroll's specific movements and attacks.

So it was in fact possible to build a training golem that mirrored any kind of monster. However, the Legion only knew how to make the owltroll version. *(It was one of their more recent discoveries.)*

79

By fighting this creature, my **skill improved** much faster than if I'd been swinging at a block with **fence arms,** like the village school kids do.

Luckily, training golems didn't have weapons, and they **pulled their punches, dealing zero damage.** I suppose that's the only reason why I managed to display any sort of bravery today.

Cobalt showed up every now and then to check on me. **He was my mentor for the day.**

I hadn't even finished my breakfast that morning when **he stormed** into the dining hall and said it was time to start my training. Normally, I might've said something along the lines of: *"Training, you say? But I am training! I'm training in the art of proper breakfast consumption!"* But instead, I just nodded and **wolfed down** my scrambled eggs.

I hadn't even questioned my consumption of scrambled eggs. **Is it odd for a cat to eat such things?** Well, how could I question a meal when I'm already wearing boots? As far as saving the world is concerned, **I'm going all the way.**

"Hurrr . . . !!" With a shout not unlike a villager's **battle cry,** the golem swung his right fist at me.

In response, I activated **Dash.**

It's a **basic ability** anyone can learn, even level 0s like me. Earlier this morning, Cobalt had given me this book called an **"ability tome."**

80

It was only five pages long, and soon after I'd read the last one, I'd gained the ability for free.

By dashing to the owltroll's left, I not only **avoided the attack** but also was now flanking my opponent. **My rapier hit its side.**

I'm . . . getting _**better**_ at this.

And that was how it went. For five hours. I must have swung a thousand times yet never managed to bring the golem's health to 0. They had really fast **regen.** I couldn't hit fast or hard enough.

That changed when Leo showed up. He let me borrow his weapons—a **katana** and a **wakizashi, both made of prismarine.** I sliced through that golem like it was butter. **Softened butter that had less resistance.**

As soon as the beast fell, I checked out my stats. **I was totally amazed.** When I'd woken up this morning, my Combat skill was at 81. And after all of today's hard work . . .

#SKILLGOALS #SUCCESS #CATMONSTER #THEHYPE #SAWBLASTLIGHTWRITELIKETHISSOIWANTEDTODOITTOO

SKILL	LVL
COMBAT	101
CASTING	0
CRAFTING	9
BUILDING	15
FARMING	7
MINING	1
TRADING	0
ENCHANTING	0

COMPETENCY	LVL
BREWING	0
FISHING	5
COOKING	0
RIDING	0
STEALTH	90
MUSIC	0
SCOUTING	88
SWIMMING	1

Dude! Look at that!

Katana
Wakizashi

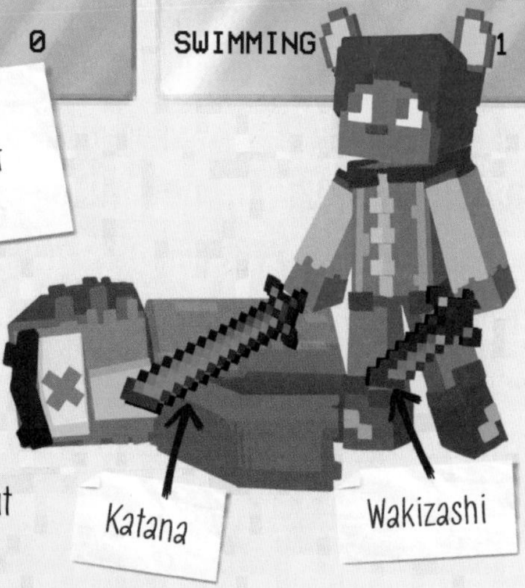

I was at 101.

Until today, I'd been ashamed of my skills. But now that I had one in the triple digits, **I could show off a little.**

Cobalt said a **twenty-point skill** increase in a single day was huge, even with a training golem. Almost a record. Leo said maybe it was because I was a monster. Like, maybe **monsters can gain faster skill increases?**

Most of my skills were still at zero, sadly. Well, my **stealth** and **scouting** weren't too bad. *(What do you expect? I'm a cat.)* As for my **swimming** skill, that's a sad story. I once fell into a river when I was a little kitten and have rarely swam since.

The golem slowly got back up, like it was coming back to life.

"Well, I think that's enough for today," Cobalt said. "**And nice work.** A skill of 101 is nothing to laugh at."

Done for today . . . I couldn't believe what he was saying. I'd seen the **ruined villages.** The whole world was crumbling. **How could I give up so easily?** I returned Leo's weapons, drew my rapier, and gave Cobalt a sidelong glance. And the way he smiled made me realize that **he'd been testing me all along.**

Of course.
There was no other way.

Battle music, 8-bit style

#FORAETHERIA

In my dreams, Kolbert was telling me something about how today **was an important day** and that I didn't want to miss breakfast. And for some strange reason, when he said that last part—**miss breakfast**—I began dreaming about literally missing breakfast. As in trying to hit my breakfast with a sword and missing it.

"Huh," I mumbled absently, without opening my eyes.

"C'mon," Kolbert said. "Let's refill that food bar of yours. Or hunger bar. Or **satiety.** Whatever you want to call it, **let's get it back to full,** because you must be starving. Then we'll head to the opera house."

"Waffl . . ."

"What?"

"**Enderpistachio pancakes** with . . . p-pineapple. Or." My eyes fluttered open. I was in my bed. "**How'd I wind up here?**"

"You don't remember?"

"Not really."

"You ended up training for eleven hours. I find that rather strange, as **I'd suggested to Cobalt that you only train for five.**"

Training . . .
The memories came **flooding** back.

Last night I had reached my goal of 125, but **did I ever pay the price.** I woke up with Exhaustion. A debuff. It reduced a number of stats, like attack speed and . . . I've forgotten the rest, probably things like strength, agility.

Not that I cared. I was more preoccupied by all the aches and pains in my arms and back—**my whole body, in fact**—which ruined my mood. Even breakfast was going to require making a decision, **aka thinking,** and I suddenly didn't want to leave my bed.

But skipping breakfast would have been **hazardous** to my health. Literally. I mean **health,** as in **hit points, HP, my life-force.** There's a stat called **satiety** that's essentially a **measure of hunger.** After yesterday, mine was in the red.

A stack of pancakes solved that issue, as well as a flask of slimeberry juice, which didn't affect my stats in any way—it just tasted really amazing. Mostly due to Steph's 152 skill in **brewing.**

Then I was escorted to the opera house. I mean, Kolbert walked in front of me, Amber and BlastLight were on either side, and Krafty was some ways behind us. **Pretty weird.** Were they my **bodyguards** or something? I immediately forgot all about that upon seeing the **cloudless blue sky.** It was the most beautiful day—sun shining down, the air filled with the cheerful songs of **blockbirds.** The villagers were pointing at them, looking delighted.

"Hoy! Blockbirds?!" An old man adjusted his glasses. "**Haven't seen one in years!**"

"Quite strange to see them here," a villager woman added. "I've read they rarely leave **Ravensong.** And why would they? **It's such a beautiful place!"**

"Mom! Dad!" A little villager girl shouted to her parents. "I saw a bat, too!"

"Oh, honey." The girl's mother gave her an endearing look. "Bats are common this time of year."

"But this one had glowing red eyes!"

Her father patted her on the head. "How about we get some ice cream?"

I wasn't sure whether that girl was telling the truth. I'd lived in a **forest biome** for years without ever seeing a bat with red eyes. But I was thankful for the blockbirds. Without them around, everyone would have been staring at **me.**

Some villagers were wearing new robes with hoods. Word on the street is Breeze's father had been teaching them a few basic spells. One spell was called **Verdant Bloom.** It sped up the growth of plants. Mostly, they'd been using this on their crops, but Bloom could make large areas of grass grow quickly and prevent the enemy from moving through them.

By the time we arrived at the opera house, the place was totally packed. There was a **huge line** outside that extended into the street.

OPERA

Krafty pointed to a large sign over the doorway.

It read *The Plight of the Terrarians* and named six Legionnaires as the play's stars. Among them were BlastLight and Amber.

He smiled at these two. "After today, you two are gonna be famous around here!"

"Not really," Amber said. "Our parts aren't that amazing. **We're just fighting some zombies.**"

BlastLight must have noticed my worried expression. "Not real ones, Eeebs. Just villagers in **zombie costumes.**"

"Oh. What about Leo?" I asked. "What will he be playing?"

"He'll be meeting Kolbert and joining the Legion. Hurion's rescuing a

87

villager from a burning house. Becca's in the final act. Her **music** skill is almost 200, so everyone asked her to sing." BlastLight wore a wistful look. "After today, she'll be the **star** of Villagetown."

Thankfully, we walked right past that long line.

Since three of the Legionnaires with us had **main roles** in the play, we had "**VIP status.**" Or so we thought . . .

As we walked up to the ticket guy—**perhaps the largest villager I'd ever seen**—he scowled and blocked the entryway. "**No cutting! Wait your turn like everyone else!**"

"Just let us in," Kolbert snapped, pointing at the large sign. "Can't you see that **we're a part of this play?**"

"Oh? Then you can show me your passes."

Kolbert turned and gave BlastLight an exasperated look. "Well?"

"**I'm looking!**" she exclaimed, frantically searching through her belt pouch inventory.

"Don't tell me you lost them," Amber said.

"They were **right here!**"

"**You really** need to learn proper inventory management," Krafty said. "That pouch is about to **explode!**" Standing next to BlastLight, he must have caught a glimpse of its contents. "**Look at all that junk!** How many random quest items do you **have?!**"

Kolbert, with his face inches from the ticket guy's, pointed back at Amber.

"See her? The one with the fox ears? **That's Amber.** How many foxtails have you seen walking around Villagetown?"

BlastLight never found the passes. What saved us was the mayor himself, who appeared in the doorway, beaming.

"Come in," he exclaimed, waving us inside. "What are you standing there for? **Come in, come in!**" I couldn't help but smile—he was dressed for the occasion, in black and red Neophyte gear.

I was the last to enter. Just before I did, a boy tugged on my sleeve. Strangely, he didn't comment on the fact that I was wearing clothes: "You **do** know you're not supposed to be walking around with your weapon drawn, right?"

"Oh, um, yes. Of course. Who **doesn't** know that?" I sheathed my rapier. "Thought I saw a slime over there. Best be careful, kid."

Kae ran up to Kolbert and saluted. He was still in uniform. "No signs of activity."

Kolbert returned this salute. "How about Ched?"

"He's guarding the balcony."

"Good. And keep an eye out, huh? Steph says she saw a **suspicious-looking** person this morning, near the west library. Judging by the description, **it's the same person** Leo saw."

Kae nodded. "I'm on it."

A villager man wearing a white apron bumped into me. A **miniature treasure chest**—half the size of a block—was hanging from a strap around his neck. He opened it to reveal a great variety of food items and flasks filled with liquid.

"Hey, man. Care for a **voidtruffle scone?** Only fifty E!"

"E?"

"**Emeralds . . . ?**"

"You mean, this stuff isn't free?"

"**Wow,**" he said with a scowl. He quickly moved on, muttering, "First the Terrarians, now this!"

"**They're here . . . !!**" By the counter, two villager girls screamed upon seeing my friends. One offered them a piece of paper identical to the poster above the door.

The other had a quill. "**C-can we get your autographs?!**"

As more villagers piled around them, the mayor grabbed my shoulder and gestured to the staircase. "I reserved an extra balcony seat," he said, "in case you decided to show. Do your best to be vigilant, Eeebs. And try to look a little **less glum,** will you?! What's the matter? You're about to witness a **grandiose saga of epic proportions,** not some trifling noob parade!"

". . . Oookay."

Before trudging up the stairs, I took one last glance at Kolbert and the rest of them.

I didn't <u>understand</u> anything.

Needless to say, it was an overwhelming experience.

I was already out of my element in Villagetown. This place was like another world. Especially the balcony. Only the **elite** were here, **including Emerald's parents.** Her mother told me about how Emerald would be heading to the capital to further her studies. News to me.

"Where is Emerald, anyway?" I asked. "I haven't seen her in a while."

The mayor cut in. "**Scouting.** She's been scouting for the past couple days. Isn't that right, Giles?"

"Indeed," said Emerald's father. "Our daughter is on a **little adventure.** She will gain some much-needed experience from her time spent in the wild. Of course, by experience I'm referring to experience points, **XP.** The mayor here felt that Emerald needed every advantage she can get, and I must say, Vera and I wholeheartedly agree."

"After all, only the **best of the best** study at the Academy," his wife said. "The competition will be quite fierce."

She offered me a gray and purple cake. It was the same thing the guy downstairs was trying to sell me. It didn't look all that appetizing. **Why are they so expensive?**

Politely declining the snack, I followed up by asking whether Runt and Breeze had gone scouting as well.

The mayor quickly changed the subject: "**Oh, thistleporridge!** I find all this talk of scouting a bit wearisome! Wouldn't you agree, Vera?"

"You need to ask?" she laughed. "Remember all the **recent attacks.** Let's talk about something a little **less dreadful,** shall we?"

The conversation went south from there. They clearly didn't want to talk about Emerald, Breeze, and Runt. But what else was I going to talk about with them? I didn't exactly have a lot in common with these people, with their **diamond-studded robes** and fifty-emerald scones.

Luckily, the lights soon dimmed, saving me from more awkward conversation.

"I suppose we should be seated, then," the mayor said.

It's about to **begin!**

> "Twas a perilous time
> for the people of Earth,
>
> To ear and eye, the w'rld
> soon come endeth,
>
> Yet thousands of players,
> all like in noobery,
>
> Did apport to a strange new
> w'rld, if not a dream,
>
> In once-virtual Aetheria,
> where we lay our scene . . ."

The show started with this simple introduction.

I don't know why Hurion was speaking like that. **Must be an Earth thing.**

Becca was at the "keyboard," which she used to produce a melody. She'd used her **music skill to interface with a block near the stage.**

After Hurion gave the audience a deep bow, **the spotlight went out.** I could see Legionnaires zooming across the stage. They replaced the backdrop of a **starry sky** with one of an ocean, and they mined all the stone blocks, replacing them with sand. When the spotlight turned back on, Amber and Leo were lying on the stage, as though asleep.

That was how many Terrarians had arrived in this world. On some remote beach in the province of **Dawnsbloom.** Others had woken up in beautiful hamlets called **sanctuaries** that had been built by dusk elves long ago and had been used as outposts. A lucky few even appeared in the streets of the capital, surrounded by "NPCs" who were just as confused as they were.

"O, we have awoken upon Dawnbloom's golden shores! So our w'rld hath not ended, as so many had believed!

Yet why have we arrived here? What glitchery is upon us in these dark and perilous times? And dearest Amber, why dost thou wear such gear of a Neophyte? Thine outfit lay in tatters, cover'd in mold!"

"Leonardios, thou wear such noobieth gear as well! To mine eye it would almost seem as thou hast climb'd from a donation pit!"

Leo brought up his status screen.

With an expression of **extreme sorrow**, he clutched his chest. "O, I have never felt such woe!" he cried. **"My abilities! My stats! All has been erased! My virtual self hath been lost!** Years of fighting monsters hadst increased my XP to a number larger than all the coins in the **royal treasury!** Alas, it is now but a single zero. What emptiness I feel! As though a piece of my soul hath been lost as well . . ."

"Hark, Leo! Do not despair, for we have truly lost nothing! **This w'rld is but an illusion! A dream, conjured by machines that rest within our very minds!** All is well, for we are still alive!"

"Indeed, you speak true! As true as the blades I once set free upon the **Eyeless One's** vile ranks and . . . ignore these ravings! What must we do?"

"We must say our goodbyes to this virtual w'rld. Upon casting the spell of **Log Out,** we will **return to the true w'rld,** as we have always done in the past. Perhaps we may return later, when the **great Entity** hath dispelled the foul glitch so plaguing this dream. . . ."

"You are right. Although I will miss this world." Wiping away an imaginary tear, Leo approached the audience.

Amber came forward as well. **"Goodbye . . . Aetheria."**

Silence.

Someone coughed.

The duo stood still like this for some time.

From what I'd heard, what should have followed was an attack from the undead. And BlastLight was to leap out heroically and save them. (They weren't actually attacked that first day. Only by nightfall did the undead arrive. The Legion had added a few embellishments.)

Leo glanced behind him and cupped his hands around his mouth: *"Goodbye, Aetheria!!"*

This time, **a silhouette emerged from the darkness.** It was dragging its feet, arms outstretched, **tattered robes** hanging from what appeared to be . . . **black withered flesh?**

A ghoul.

Someone resembling a ghoul.

The costume looked so very real.

Some of the audience must have felt this as well. **There were a few gasps.** Some kid even started crying.

Amber pulled Leo back as the figure reached for him.

'Something's wrong,' I heard her say. **My hearing had always been quite good.**

"Great," Leo said. "I left my real sword in the dressing room."

Amber and Leo drew their **basic wooden swords** intended only for the play. Then the young actors backed up to the very edge of the stage.

What seemed to be a **very real ghoul surged forward** with sudden speed, charging at Amber. **Then it stopped abruptly.**

Kae had appeared directly behind the creature, a diamond blade in each hand. He'd been invisible, having used the **Hide** ability. His concealment had been dispelled only with his hostile action.

Kae had used the **Ambush** ability, a powerful move that automatically crits, so long as your target isn't aware of your presence. **It's one of the most lethal abilities.**

The ghoul's health went from 100% to 0 in an instant. **It cried eerily and turned into a puff of smoke.**

That was when the screams began. **The panicking.** Robed figures wielding daggers had leaped up in the audience. Wisps of smoke swirled around them as they jumped onto the stage. I caught a glimpse of pink skin—**pigmen? They'd been disguised as villagers.**

Kae, Leo, and Amber turned to meet them as Lylla, Krafty, Becca, and Ghost rushed in from the wings.

Kolbert emerged from the darkness to the stage's right. "**Diamond formation!**"

At this command, the others drew closely together so that they all fought back to back. "Let's give them a free trip to the **ninety-ninth dimension!**"

The sound of diamond hitting emerald covered up the sound of the audience's screams. **All of this took place in the span of seconds.** But it felt so much longer.

I heard a scream behind me.

Emerald's mother. She'd backed up against the wall, hiding behind her husband.

The mayor, having risen from his seat, was now **staggering back,** clutching his shoulder. **Near him stood a robed creature armed with a curved green dagger.**

It was an assassin. He'd ambushed the mayor, which automatically crit him, and took two-thirds of his health in a single hit. But instead of trying to finish him off, the figure paused for just a moment.

My rapier flew. He whirled around to parry. Sparks flew next.

And upon seeing that face, I nearly dropped my sword. **The yellowish eyes. The dark green skin. The long pointed ears that drooped like wilting leaves.** Although I was quite far from attaining the coveted title of **"Monster Expert,"** I knew the creature before me was . . .

A goblin!

An actual goblin!
Here!
In the heart of Villagetown!

It was my first real battle, and my opponent was anything but basic. As we traded blows, this guy seemed to crit with every single attack. How do I know this? My VE *(visual enchantment)* made my vision **flash red and shake slightly** to let me know that I had, in fact, been crit. Thanks, **VE.** I'm glad you were there for me. How else would I have known? **The intense agony just wasn't enough.**

The mayor was just as helpful. "Get him, Eeebs!"

Get him?! Are you sure?! What do you think I'm trying to do here?!

And something wasn't adding up here. **Critical hits do more damage, right? Shouldn't my health have been lower?**

It was weird. He'd landed three crits so far, yet my health was still way above half. I glanced down at my clothes, the tunic, the leggings.

Resilience.

Poison Resistance.

It was my gear. He was dealing all crit and poison damage, and **my items had enchantments stacked to protect against both.** It seemed that the Legion had provided me with an **outfit tailor-made** for this fight. It countered his offense completely.

Was this a coincidence? It might have been seen as one, maybe, until you considered the boots. What were the odds of my encountering a goblin right after being given a pair of **goblinkickers?** About the same as sending out a lure and reeling in a cake made of frost opals, I suppose.

No, it was all too clear. . . .

The Legion had expected this. They must have known about this **specific foe,** that he'd be hunting me, and they prepared accordingly. Maybe they'd failed to anticipate a surprise attack of this magnitude, sure, but that could be forgiven. A minor oversight. **I was winning.**

Like all duels, it was a damage race. **A race my opponent couldn't win.** His health fell below a third, while mine was still above half.

His yellow eyes grew wide, **filled with panic.** He was going to run, I expected. **What else could he do?** So I was completely caught off guard when, instead, he unleashed a most **bizarre battle cry** and jumped at me, legs extended.

I had no idea what move he'd just used, but it took a chunk of my health and sent me flying back.

Of course, he had no chance of dropping me. And he wasn't trying to. He used the attack not for its damage but for its **knockback effect. A means of escape.** By knocking me into the rail of the balcony, he put more distance between us. (Kolb had once told me that the best abilities are versatile, meaning they can be used either offensively or defensively, depending on the situation.)

Then he turned and ran.

By the time I recovered, he'd run out through the double doors.

The mayor was now shaking the balcony's only real guard—**Ched**—who was sprawled across the floor, apparently asleep.

"He'll be out for a while," Emerald's father muttered. He slipped a flask with a **brilliant red liquid** into my paw. **Swiftness II.** Then he gave me a cold smile. "After him, Eeebs. You need the experience."

The battle on the stage was still in full swing, and there were still a lot of **robed pigmen.** Half the Legionnaires were in costume, including Becca in her white gown; Leo, Amber, and BlastLight in Neophyte outfits; and Kolbert in—I blinked—**a dragon costume?!**

I hadn't noticed that before. **I was so focused on the assailants.** He must have changed into the costume before the play started. Amber had mentioned that there would be a musical number before the second act that featured a number of legendary figures, including the **Dragon Prince.** It was something the mayor had requested to raise everyone's spirits.

"They'll be okay," the mayor wheezed. "And so will you. Don't let him escape. . . ."

I chugged the red liquid and ran. With a slight **woosh** the potion kicked in, and I flew past the double doors, the hallways, the counter, the entryway, and some villager in this really funny-looking zombie costume at full speed.

"Hey! Watch out! Hurrr!"

Just outside the opera house, I saw him—**a stone's throw away**—and forced every pixel of my being to go faster so I could catch up with him.

Then something weird happened. I jumped into the air, legs extended. **A flying kick, just as he had used earlier.** It must have looked so ridiculous the way I zoomed ten blocks without dropping in height, like I was flying.

My boots soon connected with my opponent, living up to their name. **That goblin went sailing, crashing in an alley near the village hall.**

By the time I got to where he'd landed, he was gone. A trip to the **ninety-ninth dimension,** I guess. In his place was a pile of yellow diamonds, three gold cookies—at least that's what they looked like—**the emerald dagger,** five **Disguise II** potions, and a black cloak with a fiery red symbol.

The yellow crystals slid across ground and flew into my body. I felt a rush. The following appeared in my vision:

$$+800 \text{ XP} - \llbracket\ 912\ /\ 2{,}000\ \rrbracket$$

It was my **visual enchantment** notifying me of XP gain: 800, **an unbelievable amount for a Neophyte.** That goblin must have been quite strong—a basic slime gives only around 25 XP.

But how'd I manage that flying kick?

So strange. It's almost like I'd copied his ability somehow. . . .

The cloak caught my eye. Its **creepy red** symbol looked like it was glowing. Looking at it made me feel uncomfortable. Of course, while I was looking at it, my **VE** displayed the cloak's basic info and stats, like it does with any item.

It had a most unusual name.

⁙⊤∷⁙⁝⁙⁙⁙ ⁙⁙⁙ ⁙⁙⁙
⁙⁙⁙⁙⁙⁙ ⁙⁙⁙⁙

ACCESSORY (CLOAK)
NIGHTWING LEATHER
UNHALLOWED

THREE ADDITIONAL ENCHANTMENTS CANNOT BE
ASCERTAINED

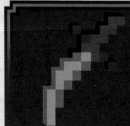

SANGUINE BLADE
DAGGER (CURVED)
EMERALD, DARK IRON
POISON II — MASTERWORK I
DAMAGE 2–5 — SPEED 0.8

GOLD DRAKKEN

Where had I seen that kind of writing before? In Lavacrest? And those cookies—who crafts cookies out of gold?

˙Eeebs! Look out!˙

I snapped to attention and saw a **ghoul** approaching out of the corner of my eye. A bolt impaled it with such force that the ghoul flew back and was pinned to a wall. That was the **Power Shot** ability. Two more bolts then found their mark, and the monster disappeared.

106

The crystals it left behind flew back toward their rightful owner, Ched.

"Not cool," I said, glaring at him. "I really need the XP. What happened, anyway? Weren't you supposed to be guarding the balcony?"

"I was. But that stupid thing hit me with **Sleep Powder** just before attacking the mayor. That was some gank, huh?"

"Gank?"

"Ah, sorry. Earth slang. **It means ambush, surprise attack.** To come out of nowhere when the enemy's least expecting it."

"Oh. So . . . is everyone okay?"

He nodded. "**All in the green. Including the mayor.** Seems Emerald's dad carries around a small potion collection. As for the party crashers, there were only a few left by the time I woke up."

"They were **pigmen,** right?"

"Yeah. **Moldsnouts. The most common type.** As basic as it gets." He kicked one of the Disguise potions. It rolled across the grass. "This guy, though . . . he belonged to the **Sanguine Brotherhood.** A guild of assassins. They jumped us before, in Morningvale. But back then, they were all wearing their guild cloaks. Not that."

He gestured toward the cloak. "**That's the enemy's sigil.** The Crying Star is this star that . . . **ah, whatever.** I don't know the lore too well." He paused, seemingly lost in thought. "How'd you take him out, anyway?"

"You didn't see that kick, I guess."

"What kick?"

"Well, it was the same move the goblin used." I opened my status system on a whim. Ched zoomed up to it so fast I had a hard time seeing my own screen. And when I did . . .

HARBINGER
CROSSBOW
SILVER, DARK IRON
DAMAGE 5–15 – SPEED 1.5
RANGE 20

PRECISION II: + 10% CRIT CHANCE
WOUNDING III: + 30% CRIT CHANCE
RAPID FIRE: AUTOMATICALLY RELOADS CROSSBOW FROM AVAILABLE INVENTORY SPACE.

I had an ultimate.

Never mind that really cool crossbow—I just got an **ult** (an abbreviation of ultimate for cool people).

I say that so casually. Let me explain. **Learning an ultimate typically involves going to a special place, like a monastery, often secluded, where one has to speak to a master capable of teaching it and train for days,** even weeks, if Kolbert is to be believed.

Yet I'd learned one without trying.

Ched stared at the screen intently. "That's so weird. I'm pretty sure **Rage of Ao** is a monster-only ability. There's also a type of **mage** that can learn them. **But I think they have to kill the monster first,** while it seems you only had to be exposed to it. Never heard of something like that."

"Hmm. I vaguely recall Greyfellow mentioning something about monster abilities. Although, I . . ."

As much as I wanted to freak out right now, I trailed off at the sight of Kolbert approaching. He was still in that **ridiculous dragon costume** and wielding that broken sword of his, the **Critbringer.**

I almost laughed.

"I should have warned you," he said. "It's just . . . the last time they attacked was so far away, and that was months ago. I really didn't think

we'd see them again. And where'd they get **Disguise potions?** Should've had more guards, I . . ."

Ched shrugged. "It's not your fault. We've all been careless."

"Yeah." That was Amber. She'd just kinda crept up on us. **I'd never seen her look so glum.** "We were just too focused on enjoying ourselves, I guess."

In the distance, Zain **burst** from the front doors of the opera house and skidded to a halt. Cobalt came out next, looking more ridiculous than Kolbert in his owltroll costume. Leo followed him, and he was running so fast he ran right into Cobalt, who went flying into Zain. **The three collapsed into a heap, their weapons clattering around them.**

"Seriously, Leo?"

"Wow. You're **such** a noober, bro."

"Yeah?! What were you guys just standing there for?!"

BlastLight stepped through the door, gave them a blank stare, and calmly walked around them. The mayor followed. He was followed by Hurion, Ghost, Lylla, Steph, Becca, Krafty, and several villagers.

"Villagetown has survived yet another attack!" he said triumphantly. "Oh, and look!" He pointed to the village hall's roof. A white bird was perched up there, watching us. It had glowing sea-green eyes. "A stormcrow! A most auspicious creature! I believe this calls for another celebration!"

Leo sprinted up to me. "I was so worried!" he shouted. He gave Ched a cold stare. "Seems the balcony was a little light on guards."

Ched returned the scowl. "Back off, novitiate. That guy was Brotherhood. Surely, you remember them."

"Now you understand why the mayor wanted you to stay with us," Kae said. He appeared out of nowhere, just like Amber. "We figured you'd be on the list."

"The list?"

"Just like we told you," BlastLight said. "Anyone linked to the Prophecy is seen as a threat."

"Yeah? Well, what kind of assassin carries around gold cookies?" I gestured to them. They were still on the ground.

Everyone around me laughed. Even Amber: "Those aren't cookies," she said, and picked one up, turning it every which way. It glinted in the light. "The drakken is the capital's official currency. They're used instead of emeralds."

Oh, right. Coins. Just like that token of Hurion's. How could I forget?

Kolbert, having **regained his composure,** grabbed one and inspected it. "Haven't seen one of these since before the—"

"Hey! Seriously?! What're you guys doing?!" It was a blonde girl named Shard, running up, looking rather shaken. She pointed to the northern sky. "We have a code green!"

Faint green bursts of light were **exploding** across the blue expanse. The slightest trail of smoke was rising below them, just over the houses. You wouldn't have seen either unless you were really looking.

That was about the time villagers came swarming from the north. Some were screaming something about the wall being on fire. Which didn't make any sense. **Stone doesn't burn.** Even I knew that.

But my friends took off running.

Despite their shouting and the mayor's yelling, I heard a voice.

■■■ *"Remember what I told you."*

It was that **elf woman;** I was sure of it. But when I looked around, she wasn't there. Either I was hearing things or she'd used some spell to communicate with me.

Follow the fire, I thought, and ran off after my friends.

Well, more like jogged, really. That potion had worn off, and I still had **Exhaustion,** which reduced my movement speed by 10%. Or was it 15%? **Possibly 12.5**—*never mind.*

I wasn't running that fast, okay?!

As I moved north, a lot of villagers came up to me.

The first was an elderly man. The very same one who'd once suggested that I had void fleas. "**Someone!! Anyone!! Save me . . .!!**" He saw me, ran over, and grabbed me by the shoulders: "**You'll protect me, r-right?! I was only joking before! You clearly don't have fleas!**"

A rotund villager man nearly knocked me over. "Hey! Cat guy! Help us out, hurrr! There's a zombie over there!"

"I'm sorry for what I said about your ears the other day!" a villager boy said. "I was just kidding! They look really cool! I swear!"

Cat guy? Better than "blue thing," I guess. And hey, what'd that kid say about my ears?! Must've missed that. But what happened to "no monsters allowed"?

"**Quit your noobering! You sound like a bunch of enderhurgles!**"

It was **Winter.** A friend of Ophelia's. Behind her was a herd of villagers. And Hurion, Steph, Ghost, and Zain. Kolbert had sent them to help Winter take everyone down into the mine tunnels, into the **Lost Keep.**

It was a good idea. They'd be safe there.

"We'll be okay," Zain said. "Help out the others, huh?"

"I'll try."

Waving, I made my way north through **Goldenglow Lane** and caught up with the others. They had just finished taking out some undead.

"Where do these ghouls keep coming from, anyway?" I heard Kae ask.

"Someone must be summoning them," Leo said. "But who? Maybe that guy we—oh, hey, Eeebs. Where were you?"

Ched shivered. He looked pale. **"Can't believe they got me,"** he said. "What a day." One of the ghouls had inflicted this magical disease called **"crypt rot."** Becca handed him a blue flask, which he chugged without hesitation or a single word of thanks. "Better."

"Glad you could join us," Kolbert said to me. **Apparently, everyone had forgotten about my Exhaustion.** "Let's roll."

The streets were completely empty by the time we reached **Aunessence.** It was Villagetown's newest district, still under construction, and the streets were lined with vacant shops. But even in this unfinished state, it was still beautiful, adorned with white quartz and light brown sandstone. Distant blocks were playing relaxing music that Lylla said sounded like wind chimes. The builders, having fled in terror just moments before, must have left the music on.

AUNESSENCE
COMMERCIAL
DISTRICT
OPENING
SOON

On our left was Becca's Bouquet, a boutique specializing in flowers with magical properties.

On our right was **Kolbert's Mystical Teahouse,** where you could get **tea** and **enchanted cookies** that looked like multicolor unicorns.

And up ahead were two Legionnaires, **Slach and Shard.** They were among those who'd missed out on the play due to **wall duty.** *(Sorry. Shard wasn't part of the Legion. She was just a friend of theirs.)* A third—named **Extreme**—arrived just as we did.

Shard ran up to a girl named **Mooncloud.** ˙I **was so worried about you! What happened?!**˙

Behind them was a fire. **A big fire.** I think that's what's called an inferno.

MOONCLOUD SLACH EXTREME SHARD

It was void fire.

The flames were so hot they made lava look like water. Scratch that, like the **enchanted water of a healing spring.** Every block they engulfed began hissing and crackling. You'd have thought that wall was made of **cookie blocks** the way it crumbled.

"I can't believe—my shop, it's . . ." Extreme was looking at a building to our left. **The Crucible: Advanced Metallurgy.** Like the wall, it was blazing with an intensity that put the Nether to shame. Even the decorative cauldrons on the roof were melting. The shop owner fell to his knees. "**I took out a loan for that!** Two thousand emeralds! And that was just the building permit! **I'm three thousand in the hole!**"

Mooncloud stepped forward. "It was **bramblemanes**," she said. "They just appeared out of thin air. Invisible, I guess. There was nothing we could do."

"How many?" Kolbert asked.

"Ten or so **mages, around level 12,** and about twenty warriors. That's including their commander. He's level 18. The rest are 7 to 9."

With a nod, Kolbert gestured to the rows of tall flowers on each side of the burning wall. "**Bush gank.** We'll find the leader and hit them with everything we've got. The others will be way easier once he's down. Krafty, you're up."

Everyone raced to find a **hiding spot.**

Kae and Becca in full stealth mode, thanks to their **Hide** ability.

In less than three seconds, Krafty and I were the only ones still standing out in the open.

I looked at him. He looked at me.

"Hey."

"Hey. Um, you should probably find a hiding spot, too."

"What about you?"

"I'm the bait."

Bait? I knew that word, but we weren't on some fishing trip.

What did Leo say about bait again? Something about these bugs called mites. You somehow attach one to your lure, and it's like getting a 25% bonus to your fishing skill, because fish will totally swarm the . . .

Oh.

Ohhhhh.

I ran so fast you'd think I no longer had Exhaustion. I hid

right next to Leo, under the porch of Daffodyll's Cafe.

Leo was dual-wielding a frying pan and spoon. BlastLight had a kitchen knife and egg whisk, Amber a rolling pin and spatula. It was ridiculous.

Some terrified villager must have dropped the utensils earlier, and the three had scavenged them. Though not meant for combat, such items could still be used as weapons and offered slightly better DPS (damage per second) than their wooden sword props.

That these three were capable of fighting with such improvised weapons only showed how skilled they really were. Later, some would jokingly refer to them as the "kitchen crew."

The wall caved in seconds later, a hole in an otherwise impenetrable defense. Here's the thing about holes in otherwise **impenetrable defenses:** bad guys pour through them. Really. They do. They see this huge smoldering rift, and they're like, "**Oh! I can run through there! Using my legs to propel me forward!**" And they just run.

There were **bramblemanes.** They're like moldsnouts, only a bit smarter, with blue skin and thick black quills instead of hair. Although some of them were mages, according to Mooncloud, the first ones in weren't. **They were warriors.**

Their leader was the first to enter. He must have been **"feeling strong,"** as they say in the Legion, because he was far ahead of all the others. He stopped upon seeing Krafty, laughed, and slowly trudged toward him.

He didn't notice anyone else. Many of us didn't have the **Hide** ability, but everyone present had a **passable stealth level**—75 or higher. Combined with the **rainbowlike foliage,** we were almost invisible to this creature, who probably wasn't very perceptive.

The flowers to his right—where Kolbert was hiding—rustled slightly.
He turned. **Grunted. Sniffed.** Then turned back to Krafty.
That was the last thing he ever did.

"... For Earth!"

The rest of us moved in, and we chunked that thing's health
bar in five seconds flat, our swords flying, Ched's bolts flying,
Mooncloud's **daggers a silvery blur, fiery cubes** hurled from
Lylla's outstretched palm—**a spell called Firebolt**—to say nothing
of Kae's and Becca's Ambush or the cooking items that **bludgeoned
and stabbed,** taking huge green chunks from his health and replacing
it with **a tiny red shining bar** all in the time it would take to say
"endermuffins." And during this **crazy barrage,** he kept bouncing up
and down like a spring, but not too high, maybe half a block, while
grunting crazily from each new hit.

"Urgurgurgurgurgurgurgurgurgu!"

At one point, his health went into the negatives. However, **his body didn't fade because of the chain of damage.** By the time he fell, his health was somewhere in the vicinity of −500%.

"That's what I call overkill."

It could be said that my friends had "**wasted**" their energy by spamming abilities on an enemy that was already dead multiple times over.

But Kolbert only shrugged. "**Kill secured.**"

We turned to face the other warriors. They had stopped in the middle of the burning wall and were **looking at one another uncertainly.** I don't know why they didn't run. I really don't. They just saw their leader take six health bars' worth of damage. If the monsters have some kind of book or guide on how to be a monster, this current situation needs to be listed in a chapter titled "**When to Run,**" on the very first line, in **bold typeface, italics, underlined, highlighted,** with at least nine exclamation points and quite possibly a sad face.

Amazingly, battle grunts soon filled the air, and the warriors resumed charging. *(I could only assume the Eyeless One was paying these guys really, really well.)*

"Uuuuurrrrrrrrrrr . . . !!" That was not a battle grunt but Extreme upon seeing the magicians hiding in the back, just past the wall. The ones responsible for his ruined shop.

"No . . . !!" Mooncloud tried grabbing him, but he dived in with **Berserk Fury**, his obsidian blades politely greeting an opponent on the front line.

And so it began.
The first **major battle.**
I'd ever seen.

At first, everything was normal.

Swords flying, allies shouting, enemies grunting. Just as I'd imagined.

Luckily, the magicians fled soon after the first one fell. We faced only warriors. Lesser versions of the one we just ganked. I took out three myself.

+100 XP — ⟦1,012 / 2,000 ⟧
+100 XP — ⟦1,112 / 2,000 ⟧
+100 XP — ⟦1,212 / 2,000 ⟧

Then I heard her voice again, calm as usual, as cool and clear as aetherglass, with the slightest crackling and hissing in the background—a noise kind of like in my dreams—coming from every direction at once, as though echoing in my mind.

▬▬▬ "Listen. Your friends are in danger. Do as I say and everything will work out."

"Where are you?!" I glanced around. The battle was raging around me. She just wasn't there.

▬▬▬ "Quick. Move left."

"**What?!**" I went to take a small step in that direction, then stopped, feeling ridiculous.

A blast of wind swept past me. It ruffled the puffed-out fur on my head. An arrow had flown past my ear. **Did the wind alter its course?**

"Was that a spell?!"

BlastLight, now fighting nearby, gave me a weird look. "No?"

■■■ "*Yes. Now, please listen. Although I can directly protect you from harm, I will do so only when necessary, to conserve my energy. Look to your right.*"

A sword came flying from the right. **A warrior, of course.** I dashed to the left then sent out a **basic thrust.** This one was a bit stronger than the rest, but I took him down with the help of BlastLight. **We split the XP.**

+75 XP — 〚1,287 / 2,000 〛

"**I don't understand!**" I shouted. "Why are you helping me *now?!* And why didn't you before?!"

I got another weird look from BlastLight, who'd retrieved the pigman's sword. "You are **so weird.**"

■■■ "*I was told not to interfere, yet . . . I could not bear the thought of what would happen if I—**Step back.**"

126

Fine.

An arrow flew past as I moved, hitting Krafty instead of me.

"Dude! What was **that,** Eeebs?! How about a little **warning** next time, huh?!"

"Sorry!!"

■■■ *"Don't worry. He'll be fine. He has much more armor than you. Move back when I tell you—go."*

Following her command, **I avoided yet another arrow.** This one came from the wall. An archer had climbed up there. Ched fired at least five times, but this enemy was taking cover behind one of the, um . . . stone things along both edges of the wall.

■■■ *"Hold on. He's afraid of loud noises. Use your breath."*

So **I coughed up a fireball.** It exploded against the stone he was hiding behind. It wasn't that loud, but he still dropped his bow and **ran like a creeper in a kitten shop,** squealing, until he fell off the wall's outer edge.

■■■ *"Good."*

"This . . . is so **insane.**"

■■■ *"Focus. **Up ahead.** Your friend will be in danger soon."*

"Which one?"

■■■ *"The blacksmith."*

Extreme? He was a bit low on health. Not too bad, though, a bit under half.

As I made this observation, **a warrior crit the Legionnaire,** who staggered back with 2 HP remaining. He cut down the bramblemane in return. There was an unpleasant noise as this enemy fell.

▪▪▪ *"Get behind him."*

After I zoomed up, **I felt something strike me in the back. It wasn't painful.** Like someone hitting me with a pillow. There was a bright flash and cracking, and wisps of smoke were swirling around me, little sparks.

Some noob just hit me with a fire spell.

Whirling around, I noticed a mage. He'd seemingly appeared out of thin air, on the edge of the battle. He'd been invisible, and this effect broke when he cast the spell. *(Which did zero damage due to my fire immunity.)*

Becca and Kae dropped him instantly, **a double Ambush.**

Extreme turned to me, shaken, and chugged a healing potion. ". . . T-thanks."

"I'm not the one you should be thanking," I said.

"Oh?"

▪▪▪ *"In five seconds, shove him as hard as you can."*

"**On** five or one second after?!"

Extreme's face looked like this: O_O "What are you talking ab—"

▪▪▪ *"Now."*

I shoved him *(as hard as I could).*

He glared at me. "Hey! **What's your problem?!**"

■■■ "*Again. Shove him.*"

I dove into him this time, **a shoulder bash,** nearly knocking him over, and I stumbled back myself.

In that moment, the look on Extreme's face was something like, "Are you **nuts?!**" But there was no time for him to actually say anything.

Three crossbow bolts hit a block of wood beside us in rapid succession: *thunkthunkthunk.* There was a spray of wooden bits and pixels, the two smallest forms of matter. The bolt had come from the roof of the **Crucible** from a goblin with a crossbow. *(How he'd fired so quickly three times in a row like that, I had no idea.)*

Ched fired in return, bolts leaving his crossbow with a loud silvery ring just next to my ear: *cling, cling.* His bow usually wasn't that loud. Was he using a particular ability? **The goblin staggered back with a bolt in each shoulder, then fell.**

Realizing what had just happened, Extreme looked at me, totally bewildered. "**Wow!**" His confusion only increased when **green motes of light** appeared around him, swirling. His health bar flew back to full. "Where'd that come from?! **What's going on here, Eeebs?!**"

■■■ "*Tell the hunter to retrieve the goblin's crossbow. It's significantly better than what he has now.*"

Hunter? She must mean Ched. Is that his class, then?

The weapon was slowly clattering down the roof, gently pushed by an **eddy of wind.** It fell into the grass nearby. I pointed to it. "**You'll wanna get that.**"

"What's going on over there?" Leo asked Cobalt.

"No idea. Since when does a level 0 quest NPC carry like that?"

I turned to a new opponent and asked in a quiet voice, "**What's your name, anyway?**"

■■■ *"Lyra."*

"And where are you, exactly?"

■■■ *"Only speak when necessary. And don't worry. We'll get through this."*

At this reply, I couldn't help but smile. **All business, huh?** I ran to meet my foe, feeling pretty strong myself. "Any tips for this guy?"

For a while there, it went just like that.

No matter what we faced, that **crazy lady** always had a plan. Clearly, she had the ability to predict the future. There was also the fact that she could speak telepathically.

Yet there were times when she chose to **"help us directly,"** as she put it.

Once, when Cobalt was surrounded, a **shimmering cube of golden light** appeared around him, shielding him from harm. **The enemy's crude weapons just bounced off it.**

Other times, a gust of wind pushed an ally from behind, increasing their movement speed, allowing them to escape from a bad situation. And **a strange green light often brought healing,** sometimes less than a second before someone fell.

Saved in such a manner, Leo looked around incredulously. "I thought I was . . ."

At times, I still looked around myself. Where was she? She seemed to be able to see the entire battlefield. Maybe she had a high vantage point? There was a large white bird perched on the roof of the teahouse. **The one from earlier.** It was watching us intently.

Wizards have familiars, don't they? Is that hers?

Whoever she was, we wouldn't have made it without her help. **There were a lot more monsters than we initially thought.**

At least thirty fell—not twenty as Mooncloud had predicted—and at least fifty more could be seen advancing through the smoke up ahead, which, by now, was almost completely obscuring the wall.

▬▬▬ *"New plan. Fall back and enter the shop just past the* **Crucible.** *You'll find good weapons in there.* **Potions, too."**

I looked that way. **The Eternal Forge,** it was called. Leaf owned that shop. It was his second. Rumor had it that he couldn't stand the thought of some Terrarian beating him at his own game, so he spent a princely sum on a fancy shop right next to Extreme's. And the rumors were true, I was sure. I overheard Leaf near the Clothing Castle the other day: "Thinks he can beat me, eh? He doesn't know who he's dealing with! I'm gonna run that little punk outta business!"

THE ETERNAL FORGE AND THE CRUCIBLE

"So there's a bunch of nice stuff in there," I said, running toward the shop. It hadn't yet caught on fire. "Why not tell me before? Would've been good to know, don't you think?"

■■■ *"I'm not omniscient. And you could say that I've been* **preoccupied.** *I only recently had the time to cast* **Locate.**"

"**Locate?** You're talking to a Neophyte, remember."

■■■ *"It reveals the location of nearby items of a type I specify."*

"Wow. **A spell that can find loot.** Please remind me to learn that the day I become a Wizard."

When I entered the shop, I nearly jumped. Leaf was in there. *Why?! WHY?!* He was cowering behind the counter, a sword in his trembling hand. "**Begone, beast!** This is masterworked steel I'm holding! **I won't hesitate to crit you where you stand!**"

133

"Leaf?!" I took a step closer. "What are you doing here?!"

He squinted. "Oh! **It's you! That blue thing!** Get out of my shop! Go find somewhere else to hide!"

"**Hide?! Really?!** What are you talking about?! In case you hadn't noticed, this whole area is burning to the ground!"

"Not **my** shop, fool! Do you see these walls?! You're looking at a double layer of **spellforged steel!** The very same as this blade! Even an army of wyrms couldn't melt it!"

Spellforged steel? **What the endermuffin is that?!** I looked around at the rough metal walls. They were adorned with a lot of frames. Some held fancy-looking weapons. So shiny.

"Oh! So **that's** why you're here! **You've come to rob me!**"

"It's kind of an emergency, all right? I mean, my friends are out—"

"Your friends! Pah! I bet they're the reason why the monsters attacked in the first place!"

"I just need to borrow them! I'll give them back! Promise!" What? **I was both exhausted and Exhausted.** It was the best I could do. "Lyra?" I whispered. "What now?"

There was no response.

"Hey," I said, louder this time. "**Are you there?**"

"Oh, I'm here!" Leaf snapped. "And **you'd** better go elsewhere, thief, if you value your health!"

"Lyra. Where are you? What do I do?!"

"Harrh?" Leaf squinted again. "Who're you talkin' to?! You crazy or somethin'?! Must be the void fleas! Heard they rot the brain!"

"Hey!" Glaring at him, I raised a finger. "I **don't** have—"

■■■ "Sorry. Tell him if he wants to save his village, he needs to let you borrow his weapons."

"If you don't lend me your weapons, **your village will be destroyed!**" Hmm. That didn't come out right. Yeah, I really messed that up.

■■■ Lyra sighed.

Leaf moved forward, scowling: "Oh, I'm afraid there's only one weapon you'll be getting!" He pointed his sword awkwardly in my general direction.

■■■ "There's no time for this."

Suddenly, to the sound of wings, **the white bird landed in the street outside.** Before its feet hit the ground, it **became pure white light and grew in height, its wings turning into arms.** Almost instantly, and without breaking stride, it **took the form of a woman.**

An elf in black robes.
**It was
Lyra.**

My mouth opened, but nothing came out.

Apparently, I could add **shapeshifter** to the very long list of **Lyra's abilities.**

Now her normal self, she entered the shop like a rapidly approaching storm. Despite this, she showed no anger, no emotion. She stopped beside me, raised a hand, and chanted.

Cubes of **pinkish-white light** swirled in the air around her.

At the same time, letters began forming above her—the same type as found on the goblin's cloak.

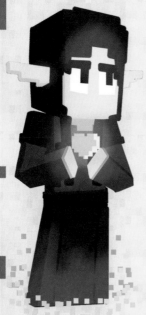

That was how most spells worked. You recited the words, which appeared above you, forming a sentence. The spell would go off when the sentence was complete.

"A **Sorceress!**" Leaf shouted. "**I should have known! Keep your distance, witch, or I'll . . .**" As he trailed off, pink motes, like little hearts, sparkled in the air around him. His anger faded, and he lowered his sword. ". . . provide you with anything you need."

"You must leave," Lyra told him. "**Run south and enter the mine tunnels.** Follow the signs to the keep. If you encounter any villagers on the way there, take them with you. If you see anything else, keep running."

"At your command." The blacksmith left the counter and ran out of his shop.

Now, imagine someone obeying an order like that. You'd find it weird. **Really weird.** But that's what had just happened.

I didn't know this at the time, but she'd just cast the spell **Charm.** While this spell was in effect, **Leaf would see her as his most trusted ally and do nearly anything she suggested.**

"Take this," Lyra said, retrieving a silver sword from the wall. "You'll need it."

FANG
KATANA
SILVER, MOON SILVER
DAMAGE 3–6 — SPEED 0.75

MASTERWORK I: SUPERIOR CRAFTSMANSHIP PROVIDES IMPROVED BALANCE AND ACCURACY.
MOON SILVER: CRITICAL HITS WILL SOMETIMES DEAL EXTRA DAMAGE.
VORPAL III: CRITICAL HITS USING THIS WEAPON HAVE A 6% CHANCE OF INSTANTLY REDUCING THE TARGET'S HEALTH TO 0 (AUTOKILL).

As I equipped this new blade, Lyra went for the door.

"I'll go back to scouting," she said. I assumed that meant **she'd return to bird form** and fly back to a roof, where she'd be able to see approaching enemies. She pointed to a chest on the counter. "The best items are in that. Take everything, including the potions. Your friends will need them."

The way I moved, **it was almost like I'd been affected by Charm myself.**

And when I opened that chest, I couldn't help but wonder where Leaf had gotten so much stuff. That chest had a ton of items, including "**flasks**" that were like upgraded glass bottles with bonus effects.

CASK OF RENEWAL
FLASK
EMERALD, MOON SILVER
CONTAINS: HEALING WATER

REFILL I: ONCE PER DAY, AT SUNRISE, WATER FROM AN ORDINARY SPRING CONTAINED WITHIN WILL BE TRANSFORMED INTO A HEALING POTION THAT CAN RESTORE 15 HP OVER 5 SECONDS. MAY OTHERWISE BE USED AS A NORMAL FLASK.

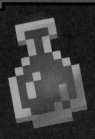

BOTTOMLESS FLASK
FLASK
DARK IRON, AETHERGLASS
CONTAINS: HEALING II (x3)

VOLUME II: FUNCTIONS AS A NORMAL FLASK, BUT CAN HOLD THREE DOSES OF ANY ONE POTION.

KING'S CHALICE
FLASK
AETHERIAN GOLD, RUBY
CONTAINS: HEALING III (+25%)

DISTILL V: FUNCTIONS AS A NORMAL FLASK, BUT INCREASES THE POTION'S STRENGTH BY 25%.

SUNSET
KATANA
SILVER, TOPAZ

DAMAGE 3-6 – SPEED 0.75

MASTERWORK I: SUPERIOR CRAFTSMANSHIP PROVIDES IMPROVED BALANCE AND ACCURACY.
INLAID TOPAZ: THIS ITEM IS MORE RECEPTIVE TO FIRE- AND LIGHT-BASED ENCHANTMENTS.
FLAMEBURST I: INFLICTS FIRE DAMAGE WITH EACH STRIKE.
BRILLIANCE I: HAS A 25% CHANCE OF BLINDING THE TARGET FOR 1 SECOND WITH EACH STRIKE. (50% IF THE TARGET HAS AN AVERSION TO LIGHT.)

DRAGON'S CLAW
DAGGER

NIGHTWYRM LEATHER, DRAGON CORAL
DAMAGE 3-6 — SPEED 0.75

MASTERWORK I: SUPERIOR CRAFTSMANSHIP PROVIDES
IMPROVED BALANCE AND ACCURACY.
DRAGON CORAL: +100% TO DRAGON ENEMIES.
CATSCRATCH I: INCREASES THE POWER LEVEL OF ANY DEBUFFS
CURRENTLY AFFECTING TARGET BY ONE POINT. (POISON I TO
POISON II, ETC.)

FULL MOON
SHURIKEN
MOON SILVER
DAMAGE 2-6 — SPEED 0.8

MASTERWORK I: SUPERIOR CRAFTSMANSHIP PROVIDES IMPROVED
BALANCE AND ACCURACY.
MOON SILVER: CRITICAL HITS WILL SOMETIMES DEAL EXTRA DAMAGE.
BOOMERANG: UPON STRIKING A TARGET, RETURNS TO ITS OWNER'S
HAND OR INVENTORY.

STINGER
CROSSBOW
SILVER, SPIDER SILK
DAMAGE +2 — SPEED 1.35

ARM MOUNT: THIS WEAPON MUST BE ATTACHED TO A GAUNTLET. IT
WILL NOT OCCUPY A WEAPON SLOT BUT FIRES NORMALLY.
RAPID FIRE: AUTOMATICALLY RELOADS CROSSBOW FROM AVAILABLE
INVENTORY SPACE.

KOKO'S CANE
STAFF
MOON-FIRE WOOD

DAMAGE 2–12 – SPEED 2.15

MOON-FIRE WOOD: THIS ITEM IS IMMUNE TO FIRE.
STONEWEAVE V: INCREASES THE STRENGTH OF EARTH SPELLS
CAST BY 10%.
HOPEWEAVE V: INCREASES THE STRENGTH OF BLESSINGS
(BUFFS) CAST BY 10%.
LIFEWEAVE X: INCREASES THE STRENGTH OF HEALING
SPELLS CAST BY 20%.
REPLENISH II: +10% MANA REGENERATION.

CRESCENT
WAKIZASHI
SPELLFORGED STEEL

DAMAGE 5–8 – SPEED 1.1

MASTERWORK I: SUPERIOR CRAFTSMANSHIP PROVIDES IMPROVED
BALANCE AND ACCURACY.
SPELLFORGED STEEL: DURABLE ALLOY RESISTANT TO FIRE AND
MAGIC. THIS OBJECT DOES NOT PROVIDE A PARTICULAR RESISTANCE
TO ITS WIELDER, BUT IT RESISTS SPELLS THAT COULD IMPACT IT
DIRECTLY (SUCH AS HEAT METAL).

"Eeebs?!
Where were you? And
where did you find
all that stuff?"

(There were other weapons with enchantments I'd never seen, but I spammed enough.)

My friends wasted no time grabbing the loot.

And Lyra wasted no time giving me a new order.

━━━ *"Good work. You've turned this battle around. Now head south."*

"As in, leave the battle?"

━━━ *"Yes. Three mages are approaching your party from behind."*

"Where? I don't see them."

━━━ *"Oh. Sorry."*

A white glow surrounded my vision. That was **Wizard Eye,** a spell that allowed me to see through magical concealment. Three robed pigmen came into view fifty or so blocks away, two in red and one in black, just past the teahouse.

"They're . . . going to gank."

■■■ *"That's right. To prevent this, you'll need to intercept them and create a diversion."*

"And how exactly am I supposed to do that?"

■■■ *"I gave you that sword for a reason. Use your imagination."*

"*My imagination is not that great,*" I wanted to say, along with, "*Maybe I should get some help instead of attacking a group of fire-wielding wizard things by myself.*" But my friends had to hold the wall.

I dived in without a thought, **like a noob** diving into an **enchanted wishing well** with diamonds at the bottom. But I don't think those actually exist. And people would probably toss in emeralds, not diamonds. Also, a noob would dive in with glee, while I was quite nervous. You know what? Never mind.

"Hey! Eeebs!" Kolbert called out. "Where are you going?!"

Sprinting as fast as I could—my arms and legs moving like crazy—I looked back at him and shouted: "I'm just doing what I'm told!!"

They all gave me disconcerted looks as I ran off.

And I heard BlastLight mutter, "So weird."

(Incredible, huh? My hearing is really *amazing*.)

As I charged toward my enemies, they almost ran. You could tell it was the first time they'd ever encountered a **humanoid cat** who could see through their **invisibility spell.** They just had this whole, "What is that thing, why is it running at us, and how is it able to see us?" vibe about them.

■■■ *"Don't worry about their spells. You'll be fine. Just facetank them."*

"Face what?"

I did, of course, question the wisdom of rushing into a group of creatures whose sole purpose in life seemed to be burning everything in sight. **But only for a second.** Because back at the wall, if Lyra hadn't been there, I would have taken so many arrows I would have turned into a pufferfish. So how could I question her now?

The mage in front began casting as I drew closer.

Despite using **Dash,** I couldn't reach him.

Whatever spell he'd cast was fast-acting. The words appeared almost instantly, and a **cube of flame** sprang from nothing. . . . **The impact stopped me in my tracks.** More spells flew, and a cone of purple flames engulfed me, followed by a spray of **orange** flames, a stream of **blue** flames, and a skull of **green** flames that howled as it flew at me.

Yet, despite this **colorful assortment of flames** that destroyed part of the column behind me, **I emerged alive and unharmed.**

So that's what **facetank** *means. I get it now.*

With an irritated grunt, the black-robed pigman stepped before the other two. "He is of boss man prepared us about! Beast of come true story! **Fall him!**"

His comrades seemed just as bewildered as I was at this failed attempt at speech.

Scowling, the one in black then pointed at me, shouting something in an unknown language. Weirdly, I was able to comprehend what he'd said. Something about **killing the cat man, the foul vermin must die.** And somehow I knew that was **ancient Aetherian,** a language used thousands of years ago. . . .

I was expecting more flames at this point, but no. With a horrible screech, a **torrent of meteors** flew from his hands, **red and orange and yellow.** Apparently, he'd used some ultimate spell.

The other two joined in, casting the same exact ult, **Meteor Storm.**
I must have been hit a hundred times.

The things I do for my <u>friends.</u>

Facetank /festæŋk/
Verb. Third person.
Present: He facetanks.
Present perfect: He
has facetanked.
Simple Past: He facetanked.

1. To take the brunt of an enemy's attack without attempting to avoid it, relying instead on one's defense.
Example: "That crazy Eeebs just totally facetanked three ults."

Five seconds
later . . . *Horrible
scream grows louder*

Angry shouting in ancient Aetherian
that I don't know how I understood:
"That elf must be protecting him!"
"M . . . Mister?! We can't hold out much
longer! We're going to run out of mana!"
"Keep going, you noobs, or you're
going to run out of life soon!"

Ten seconds later . . .

"Mister?! His defenses are still holding! He hasn't sustained any damage! Are you sure it's some kind of protection?!"

"What else could it be?! Look at his gear! He doesn't have any fire resistance!"

"But . . . but he . . ."

"**Don't stop!**—You know what will happen if we fail! And never mind what those moldsnouts say. There is no glory in being fed to **enderhurgles!**"

I didn't learn this until later, but **Meteor Storm** is a "channel" spell. The spell is continuous; it keeps going for as long as you stand in place, channeling. And each second of channeling drains your energy, or mana, or whatever it's called—**I'm no Wizard.** They ran out of juice roughly fifteen seconds in.

The screaming gave way to silence. I opened one eye. Then the other. Then I looked around the gray fog and reached up to feel my eyebrows. *They're still there. My whiskers, too. Huh.*

Amazingly, **I hadn't taken a single point of damage.** The same couldn't be said for the surrounding area, though—it was in total ruins, filled with smoke and red flames. Each meteor had left behind void fire. Behind me, **Becca's shop had been completely obliterated,** and past that was a reddish glow.

Leaf's place. So much for his spellforged steel . . .

Suddenly, everything made sense. **Follow the fire.** That had been Lyra's plan all along. With **my immunity,** I was the perfect weapon against these guys. I'd made them waste spells that would have **annihilated** my friends.

I couldn't see the mages anymore, but I'd heard their footsteps as they turned and fled.

A blast of wind then swept through the street, whisking the smoke away.

■■■ *"After them. In seven seconds, your ultimate will be off cooldown. Use it as a gap closer."*

My ult. I'd forgotten all about it.

But what'd she mean by "gap closer"?!

"Can't you just speak like a normal person?!"

I tried activating my ult, **Rage of Ao,** but I must have made some mistake, because screens appeared, cluttering my vision. It seemed like information on the ability itself.

Another woman's voice, cold and emotionless, echoed in my mind:

『*Your visual enchantment's battle prompt has been enabled.*』

When I tried activating rage again, the voice mentioned something about a cooldown.

『ABILITY IN COOLDOWN!
3.5 SECONDS LEFT! 』

RAGE OF AO
TYPE: TECHNIQUE (ULTIMATE)
MANA: 75
RANGE: 10
COOLDOWN: 20 MINUTES

A KICK THAT SENDS USER FLYING 10 BLOCKS, OR
UNTIL CONTACT WITH AN ENEMY. THE FIRST TARGET
HIT RECEIVES 20 DAMAGE (AND IS KNOCKED BACK
10 BLOCKS). ALL ENEMIES THE TARGET COLLIDES
WITH WILL TAKE AN EQUAL AMOUNT OF DAMAGE. ALL
DAMAGE INFLICTED BY THE RAGE OF AO IS CONSIDERED
CRITICAL DAMAGE.

149

I didn't know how I made all of this appear. **I'm such a noob sometimes.**

"Warning," the voice said in a monotonous tone. "Your **satiety is very low.** You need food badly."

"Lyra?! My VE's **spamming** like crazy! I can barely see anything! I think it said something about a battle prompt?!"

■■■ "Your battle prompt? How'd you manage that? It's normally inactive and reserved for training purposes. Meditate upon the keyword 'disable.'"

Meditate? What kind of fancy word is that?! Disable. **Disable!**
DISURBBBBLLEEEE!!!!!!!!!

『 *Your battle prompt has been disabled.* 』

The screens fell away. I meditated again on my ultimate, hoping I'd actually get it right this time. I felt a rush as I leapt into the air and—

flying toward the closest mage—realized what Lyra had meant by closing the gap.

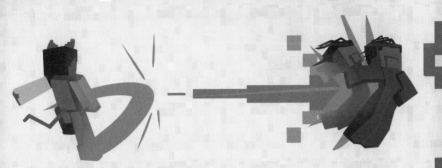

I sent one of the **gentlemen in red** flying. He smashed into the other, and both fell. Their leader didn't even try to help them. He just ran away.

Before I could finish them off, though, someone charged in from the side, shouting at the top of his lungs. **It was Drill,** in a suit of brown metallic armor and wielding a huge warhammer. He ran in and stole my kills. What a guy. I got some XP from that, since I did most of the damage, but still.

+90 XP — 〖1,377 / 2,000〗
+90 XP — 〖1,467 / 2,000〗

"Nice job!" he boomed. "Guess the mayor was right, after all! You really are Villagetown's secret weapon!"

■■■ *"Ignore him."*

"Gladly." I began sprinting south again.

To my right, armed villagers began pouring out of an alleyway, most no older than thirteen.

"What part of **head to the square** didn't you understand?!" I heard Drill shout at them. "The lot of you are as useful as an **anvil boat!**"

My ult was on cooldown again, **but the cooldown on Dash was only fifteen seconds,** so I activated that . . . and zoomed forward a mere two blocks. This did little to **"close the gap"** between me and the black-robed pigman, who seemed to be slipping away.

"Don't suppose you can do anything about this **Exhaustion?** It's lowering my movement speed by . . . wait, how much does it lower one's—"

With a soft green light, my Exhaustion wore off. Lyra had used a spell called **Revitalize.** She followed up with **Grace of Elune.** It's one of the basic "buff" spells all wizards can learn and increases your movement speed by 20%.

No longer exhausted, and pushed by magical wind, I nearly caught up to the magician before he fled into one of the staircases going to the mines. **A wall of lava bubbled up behind him,** blocking the way.

He'd used the **Magma Field** spell. The lava it conjured didn't move and couldn't be **extinguished or dispelled in any way.** One could walk through it, although anyone noob enough to do so would take a massive amount of fire damage. *(Unless said noob was me and immune to fire.)*

I still hesitated, having noticed a **red glow** in the distance over the houses.

There must have been a fire. That wasn't too surprising—only this fire had to be near the center of the village, not the wall. **The whole village is burning.** A low, eerie howl was coming from that direction. Not of any person or animal, but something unnatural . . .

▬▬▬ *"You'll have to take it from here."*

"You're . . . **leaving?"**

▬▬▬ *"I'm afraid I have no choice. Immunity to fire is a luxury I don't have. We'll meet again, of course."*

And just like that, Lyra flew off.

"**But you can't leave now!** Maybe you hadn't noticed, but **I'm nothing without you!"**

▬▬▬ *"That's a lie. You'll be fine. And there are others who could use my assistance right now. Find him, Eeebs. Don't let him reach the village folk. We can assume that's where he's headed."*

"B-b-but—"

Vanishing behind the houses, she left me with one last pearl of wisdom.

▬▬▬ *"And look to your right."*

I slowly turned, expecting to see yet **more monsters.** It was something worse, however, much worse—**Drill and Kae had finally caught up to me.** Becca, Slach, and BlastLight were behind them. Kolbert must have sent them to check on me. That meant the wall up north was holding.

153

Drill smiled as he approached. **The first time since we'd met.**

Noting the crackling wall to my left, the angry villager backed up. "That one's their leader?"

"Do you really think I know what's going on?"

Becca skidded to a halt and gave the wall a thoughtful look. "Why do I get the feeling you were meant for this situation?"

Zain came running up just then, looking quite terrified. "Mayor's down. **Permasleep.** And the west wall was breached. We've already rounded up most of the villagers, though, so Lucie wants all of us to regroup south of the square. They're building a wall there as we speak."

"A last stand," said Slach. "Is that it for bad news, or . . . ?"

Zain turned his head slightly, as though suggesting we look behind him. "Not exactly."

Past him, a number of people were approaching. Well, from this distance, they looked like people—humans with really **pale skin, tattered clothes**—but I couldn't help noticing the way they **shambled,** their outstretched arms, and their jade-colored eyes.

"**Wights**," Drill spat. "I'd tell you folks I've seen worse, but that'd be a lie."

BlastLight moved in behind him. "I hate to say it, guys, but this might be the day the ice cream stand begins serving only one flavor."

Drill laughed nervously. "What are you talking about?"

"Um, weren't you the one who said if the **monsters** ever took control of this place, they'd serve only **slimeball-flavored ice cream?**"

"Must've been Runt. Sounds like something he'd say."

Without a word, the others readied their blades. Their silence said more than words ever could.

Wights are pretty terrible, I guess. I'd read about them in one of the Lost Keep's libraries the other day—*History of Aetheria: Volume XII*. It mentioned something about how zombies are merely the reanimated, mindless, while **a wight is driven by power from a darker realm.**

That book also mentioned "**unliving energy**," how they possess a lot of it and how they **could sap the life essence from their victims with a single touch.**

In **noobspeak,** any damage inflicted by a wight results in **XP** drain. Of all the nasty powers a monster could have, there's literally nothing worse.

"We'll handle this," Becca said. "Go get the mage. The last thing we need is for him to come back with full mana."

155

I wasn't about to argue. If I was drained to 0 XP, **my level would be reduced,** and that would make me level −1. Was that even **possible?** Could I really become even more of a noob than I already was?

I did **not want** to find out.

The mage had a good head start, but **I had Lyra's wind spell boosting my speed,** along with a really good nose. To find him, I only had to follow it. So I did. All the way to some side tunnel.

I carefully sniffed the air. He definitely went in there, all right. So he wasn't going to the Lost Keep? **How strange.**

A sign nearby read as follows:

> NO TUNNEL
> ~~TUNNEL 67~~
> OFF LIMITS

Tunnel 62?

Oh, no, that's not a 2.

*Yeah, that's actually a . . . w-wait. **67?!***

So he went into—I mean, he . . .

why would he—

(? ? ? ? ? ? ? ? . . . ? ! ? ! ? ! ? ! . . .

(unintelligible chirping sounds))

0

0

.

"[o<0]"
//[ ]\\<   ← *(I must have looked like this.)*

This was the moment everything changed. The moment I realized there was more to this attack than anyone knew. The moment I **looked like a confused blockbird.**

Why would he go in there?! Does he have some kind of death wish?

This wasn't some random tunnel he'd entered, **like number 68, with its little pool of lava at the end.** This was a tunnel you couldn't even mention without some villager's face turning white. I'd once asked a shopkeeper about it. His response: *Nope, never heard of it! And no more questions! In fact, I'm closing my shop early today! Suddenly feeling a bit tired! So strange! Good day to you, sir. Good day!*

Yeah, there was a reason why they'd sealed this place off with **five layers of stone.** But now, what little remained was crumbling, and a **pool of blue lava** was oozing from the floor.

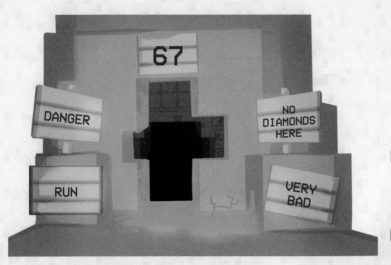

Or maybe it was slime. **Its blue light pulsed eerily,** and up close you could hear it breathing. Whatever it was, **it was dissolving the stone** around it at an alarming rate.

Faster than mining through it, I suppose, and nowhere near as loud. So maybe this was their plan all along? Yeah, he sure seemed to know where he was going, didn't he? But what's down there? What's he after?

Determined to solve this mystery, I leapt across the pool with a Dash.

In the halls ahead there were **shining blocks of copper** and **rows of small geometric shapes carved into sandstone.** Another weird and ancient language, most likely, and a strange sight to be sure . . . But the chamber ahead was even more strange.

Back in my kitten days, when I'd first stumbled across that portal, it had seemed ancient. This place seemed even older.

The Halls of Agemmon. Who was he, how is his name pronounced, and why do his halls exist **beneath Villagetown?** These are mysteries that wise men will someday ponder in Kolbert's mystical teahouse over mugs of noob's respite *(a flavor of tea, or so I've heard)*.

The pictograms made me recall another book I'd read: *The Abecedarian Dungeoneer.* One page was dedicated to pictograms called **dungeon script.** Each symbol represented some hazard or aspect of the area ahead.

The one that looked like a crescent moon meant this place contained at least one **"Safe Zone"** where one could rest without being attacked. The skull with a bone meant undead were present. I couldn't remember the rest.

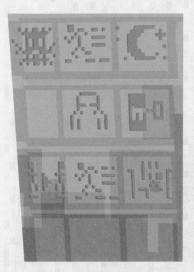 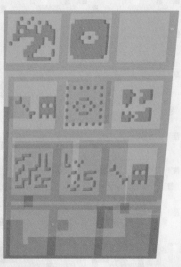

Some of the inscriptions were clear: **someone running, someone falling.** Maybe they indicated different types of traps. But I had no idea why some were displayed twice, and as for the rest . . . Well, what could an **eye surrounded by a dotted line** possibly mean?

I paused at "Lv. 35."

Does that mean . . . the monsters in this area are that level?

That was when I noticed the floor. Specifically, the ruby blocks set into it. *Huh. Y'know, that almost looks like . . .* I backed up so I could see the whole thing. *Oh.*

Suddenly, I was no longer thinking about mysterious inscriptions. The only real mystery now was why I hadn't yet run away. I'm a curious cat, but I'm wary of anything decorated with the **Crying Star,** the Eyeless One's favorite symbol.

"Lyra? Can you hear me?"

No response. *(Perhaps I was too far underground.)*

Well, she told me to take care of that mage, I thought, *and given how he just ran into a place like this all by himself, let's assume he's already been taken care of.*

I turned around, ready to leave. Then I heard the **faintest** sound and stopped. A distant shout came from farther within. It sounded like **"Nova,"** EnderStar's true name.

Well, I thought, *maybe I'm more curious than I realized. What am I*

talking about?! I know what curiosity did to the cat! I must . . . resist
. . . the urge . . . to find out . . . what's—

I zoomed through the entryway. Totally unprepared for what I was
about to see.

All I can say is if those halls really had belonged to some person
named **Agemmon,** he must have surely been a king. . . .

Vast columns of stone and copper as far I could see—more of a maze
than any dungeon. Or some **abandoned, underground** city. I gazed
upward in awe, forgetting all about why I'd come here in the first place.

Even with my respectable **stealth,** my boots were loud against the
stone floor. *So quiet. And it's . . . brighter than I expected. This room
must be two hundred blocks across. Who could have built such a thing?
And where'd they get so much copper?*

Despite the chamber's enormity, I felt that it was just the smallest fraction of a much larger complex. That **a labyrinth** of this size could exist beneath a place like Villagetown— **it was simply mind-boggling.**

It made me feel so tiny and insignificant—and not only physically. You could feel the weight of history in this place. It must have held **legends** in its blocks of stone. There must have been a reason it existed, and why it had been forgotten, and I began to imagine what it must have been like to have lived here during its **heyday,** the halls filled with now **long-lost races** of creatures. . . .

Who had they been? What had happened to them? There was so much about this world that I simply did not know. And, suddenly, I recalled reading something about this place, something about "**fire dwarves. . . .**"

I heard the sounds of battle in the distance. So I kicked off through the countless columns, following the noise.

Before long, it would be hard to find my way back. Every path looked the same, and it was getting darker— **the lanterns were becoming less and less common.**

I picked up speed as the **clangs of metal** grew louder. Behind one of the columns was an **epic sight.**

Two knights were battling in a gloomy expanse. One was a **bramblemane in polished black armor.** His sword looked like it was made of fire, and his cloak looked like a fallen red star.

The other was completely covered in interlocking gold plate, including a full helm. It would have been easy to mistake him for a **golem.** His orange cloak had a glowing emblem of a blazing sun. Sparks were flitting and dancing over its surface.

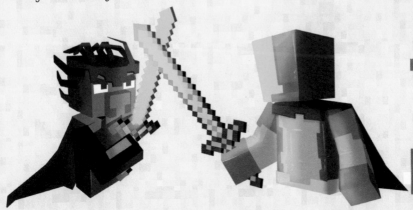

Past them, mages had gathered around a black metal object filled with violet flame. The mage I'd been chasing was among them. Another was tossing assorted reagents—**powders, bat wings, mushrooms**—into the flames. **They grew brighter with each one.**

The knights fought without acknowledging them in the least.

I watched in awe as their **blades clashed** endlessly with an unnatural sound. Yet, despite their duel's intensity, with movements almost too fast to follow, neither was struck by an opposing blade nor showed any sign of fatigue. **There could be no victor.**

Perhaps understanding this, the knight in gold fell back. He lowered his sword.

His opponent did the same. "**You've come a long way,**" the pigman said. "To think that just months ago, you were wandering around the capital without a **drakken** to your name."

"Our kind is nothing if not resourceful," the one in gold replied. Before he spoke, I'd assumed that he was an ally. But his voice gave me the **total chills.** It was deep, hollow, with a slight metallic ring. "Yet I suppose even the denizens of this world can be rather inventive—from time to time." He glanced at the mages, who were still surrounding the violet flame, which now gave off a sky-blue light. "So this is Nova's brilliant plan. **Ritual magic.** A flock of uninitiates hunched over a brazier."

The bramblemane laughed. "**Since when did you start talking like an NPC?**"

"Since when did you obey one? The Exile gave you that quest, and off you went. I'll bet you even bowed."

"It's a quest chain, actually."

"So I've learned. Assisting with the attack on **Diamondhome.** Spreading plagues through animals. You've been so busy these past few weeks."

"Yeah, it's been hard," said the bramblemane. "But I'll be resting soon enough. This is the quest chain's final segment. '**The Village Will Burn,**' it's called." The black knight smiled. "You can imagine the requirements for its completion."

"But to what end?" the gold knight asked. "What is your motivation? Is the reward so great?"

"It is. **Priceless, in fact.** Once the village falls, I'll be given access to the strongest class known. The NPCs call them **vocations,** don't they?"

"And which vocation are you referring to?"

"Oh? You haven't been doing your research. Guess you'll find out the next time we meet."

They'd moved around during their banter, and when the **gold knight** turned a little more, I could finally see his helmet. At least, I **hoped** it was a helmet.

Looking at him, "good" was the last word that came to mind—"ally" a close second to last.

Luckily, neither knight seemed to have noticed me. I'd moved back behind one of the columns and was peeking around it while using **Creep.**

"By the way, that's some nice armor," the bramblemane said. "You must've picked it up in **Silverfall.** That's the only place I know of with **craftsmanship** like that." He smirked. "Should've known you'd like spending your time with **moon elves.**"

"Only a fool would discount them," the gold knight said. "You would not believe how much knowledge they still possess."

"Not like it matters." Black threw his blade into the scabbard at his side. "Now that **the Unseeing** has **Nova's full support,** he's already won this war."

The gold knight laughed. A metallic shudder. "**Has he?**"

"I could tell you more, but you'd need to join our ranks."

"As interesting as that might be," the gold knight said, "my stance on all of this has not changed. I promised to protect the people of this world. This world is real, and those you call **NPCs are real people.** People I am sworn to protect."

"So be it." **The pigman** backed up toward the mages. "Tell Lyra I said hello, huh?"

The gold knight stepped forward. "Don't be a fool, **Bayliss.** You know how I must respond should you attempt that spell."

"Yeah, I know. But I think it's better if you just watch." With that, a **ring of shadow** flew from the pigman's hand. It wrapped around the gold knight, binding him in place. It seemed the gold knight could no longer move, or even speak. He struggled to break free.

The pigman turned his back on the gold knight, faced his subordinates, and nodded. Together they began **chanting, intoning, almost singing.**

Suddenly, with a low rumble, a **maelstrom of ghostly blue light** formed between them, swirling, and large runes appeared in the gloom above them. It seemed they were casting together. A combined effort to unleash some powerful spell.

I crept from my hiding spot to get a better look.

The chanting grew louder. Something about **answering, heeding a call—an awakening.**

Well, I didn't need to be a Wizard to know that something truly bad was about to happen here. And I knew I had to stop them. I just . . .

wasn't sure how. I knew charging in would have meant the end of me. **And I couldn't attack, even if I'd wanted to.**

I couldn't move forward at all.

A large sword was blocking the way, its broad side snug against my chest. The gold knight's eerie voice murmured to my left.

·You should not be here.·

He had **broken free** from
that spell and slipped toward me.

Then with a short cry, he spun—yes, spun—toward the enemy, leaving behind red afterimages as he did. The **Spin Dash** ability let him travel ten blocks in a fraction of a second.

"Spin Dash" . . .
Who comes up with
these names?

Is there a Wizard whose only
job is to officially name
things? How does that work?

That first mage fell so fast. **Boom,** after two swings back to back. Even so, the others didn't turn around—they were so focused on completing that spell.

The gold knight worked his way around them, relentless, his **greatsword the speed and color of lightning,** each strike with a **peal like thunder.** They fell and fell until there were no mages left except for Bayliss.

By now, the maelstrom was **swirling violently,** and the runes overhead had nearly formed. I joined the gold knight in attacking the knight in black. It was like swinging at a bedrock wall. Most of my strikes did 0, the rest no more than 1.

How much armor does he have?!

He just kept casting, though, even with the two of us **hammering away.** His health fell ever lower while the vortex grew and grew.

The gold knight hesitated before what would be a final swing. **"This is your last chance!"**

But Bayliss, filled with anguish, never stopped uttering those words. At last, **the golden blade fell.** However, at the exact moment his health reached 0—

=)\F R=7LFU\R=)F⌐UR=FLTU\R⌐⌐(\))F,\R⍳FU R⌐?U⌐7)⌐ � I⌐H

—the spell formed a complete chain.

A loud noise rang through the hall. **I jumped, startled,** looking around. Nothing had changed. The spell had only made a lot of noise. That was it. When I turned back, Bayliss had fallen to his knees.

He looked up at the gold knight. "Glorm, you . . . shouldn't have hesitated, huh?"

"You should have never begun."

"Yeah. I know. Here's hoping you're wrong, and it really is just a dream. . . ."

His form, freezing completely, turned **light blue and transparent,** fading, vanishing to nothing. **Only crystals remained.**

+125 XP — ⟦1,592 / 2,000⟧

The golem-like knight lowered his head. Although I couldn't see his face, **I noticed the way he trembled.** It seemed they'd once been close.

The deep chime was still echoing in the distance.

Shuddering once more, the gold knight turned to me at last. "We must leave and warn the others," he said, "or many more will perish. **I'm afraid Villagetown is lost.**"

I was still so stunned by what had happened. It took me a moment to respond. "Why? That spell didn't seem to . . ."

"That was a ritual spell known as **Rite of Awakening. It rouses all negatively attuned beings within two thousand blocks, alerting them of prey.** For most settlements, this wouldn't be a significant threat. However, with Villagetown so close to the labyrinth . . . you could think of it as being built on a volcano, with that spell leading to its eruption. **Only, instead of lava . . .**"

As he spoke, I saw a shambling form creeping up behind him. A zombie. "Hey." I pointed, but there was no real need. The **creature collapsed,** bursting into flames.

That was not the result of some crazy ability or spell but . . . the gold knight's fiery cloak.

DAWNBLAZE CLOAK

SILVER, FIRE
ELEMENTIUM

LIFE +8

ARMOR +10

MAGIC RESISTANCE V

FIRE RESISTANCE V

POCKET II: **CONTAINS TWO
INVENTORY SPACES.**
FLAME WREATH: **ALL HOSTILE
ENTITIES IN A 5-BLOCK
RADIUS GET 5 FIRE DAMAGE
POINTS PER SECOND.**

So Kolbert wasn't
kidding. **Gear is life.**

Glorm glanced behind him, without showing interest. "The weakest among them," he said. "And the first of many. At this very moment, every last aberration within this labyrinth is rousing from a dormant state."

"**Aberrations** are . . . ?"

"**Negatively attuned life.**"

"Um."

"What you would call monsters."

What is up with these people and their crazy words?!

"How many?"

174

"Hundreds, perhaps. Very likely more than the Legion can handle. **The clan is quite under-leveled.**"

"You can stop them, though, right?"

"Unfortunately, I can't face them alone."

Someone called out from behind us, "You'll try anyway, though, won't you?"

No, not "someone." **Lyra.** I never felt more relieved at hearing **Ms. Cryptic's voice.**

But the gold knight seemed irritated. "**Where were you?**"

"**The Legion needed my assistance.**"

"And why would you not inform me?"

"I can't message through stone," she said, meaning **her telepathy.** "You should have told me what you were about to do before you left the surface."

The gold knight shrugged. "I went to check on the village folk. Felt something was amiss."

"And something was, it seems." Lyra was staring at the black metal object. **It no longer held any flame.** "A brazier. So they—"

"**Rite of Awakening,**" Glorm replied. "Nova's latest attempt to win the Unseeing's favor, if Bayliss is to be believed."

"**Bayliss? He's here?**"

"No longer."

"You mean . . . ." Lyra's face darkened.

Mine, too. "I don't understand," I said. "Why did that guy . . ."

"His actions were based upon the belief that what we are now experiencing is merely an anomaly, an **aberrant state of mind.** An understandable view. For my kind, it is much easier to think of this world as anything but reality."

A hiss echoed in the distance.

Lyra glanced in that direction. Past the glow of lanterns, **there was only darkness.** "Do we stay?"

"That would be our duty," Glorm said. "At the very least, we will buy the village time. Of course, we must inform the Legion of what's coming."

"I'll need a recipient," said the elf.

"Kolbert. He is their leader. Tell him the seventh chapter has come to pass. He will understand."

At this, a **spectral bird appeared in Lyra's hands.** Holding the animal closer, she whispered something into its ear, and it flew away, toward the surface, I assume. *(Was it a Message spell?)*

I gave both of them an exasperated look. "Okay, I know you're here to help, I get that, but . . . **who are you people?! Who?!**"

"We were sent by our **guildmaster,**" Lyra said, "to observe the enemy's progress. He warned us not to interfere. However, there were . . . complications."

Of course, she didn't actually answer my question. Who are they?! I got the feeling they were from Earth, but why did they keep talking like that? Well, there had been times when Kolbert spoke in much the same way. What'd he call it? "**Role-playing**"?

The gold knight was staring at me. I felt the **greenish wells** of his eyes inspect my very soul. "We left Silverfall only to encounter a rider bearing a quest orchestrated by the king himself. A quest that called for the protection of settlements across the east. A **strange predicament,** then, was upon us. Our guildmaster had told us not to interfere with the affairs of the people of this world. To heed our master's warning was to ignore this country's lord."

Lyra nodded solemnly. "It was only when we saw the flames that we finally made a choice."

"And now it is you who must choose," said the gold knight. "Returning to your friends would be a wise decision. Yet I believe you would have more to gain by remaining here." He raised an armored hand. "**A quest can be shared. A kitten can decide.**"

"Is it important?" I asked.

"Through its completion, you will obtain a reward in the form of **wealth and power,** both of which you sorely lack."

His hand moved slightly to the right.

A quest invitation screen appeared before me.

GLORM HAS INVITED YOU TO JOIN
THE FOLLOWING QUEST:

『 A CALL TO ARMS 』
HELP ELIMINATE 100 MONSTERS
NEAR ANY SETTLEMENT EAST OF
MORNINGVALE. [DETAILS]

ORCHESTRATORS:
KING RUNEHAMMER II
GRAND MAGISTER ALFRIC

REWARD:
800◊
2,500 XP

ACCEPT   REFUSE

I sighed. "You know, I'm still having a hard time wrapping my head around this quest stuff."

"What you're looking at is nothing more than a **magical contract**," Lyra said. "Should you accept, you'll be bound to complete it. It would be wise to do so. In truth, it is an easy task. Although you are **currently weak, under-leveled,** you will only need to stay near us. We will cover you."

178

Cover me . . . It sounded like they were going to do all the work. So I only had to stand around, watching them, and I'd **earn a reward? Eight hundred emeralds and 2,500 XP?!** *Sign me up!*

The way my paw flew toward that "accept" button I'm surprised I didn't inflict actual damage to the screen. The screen fell away with a cheerful sound, *bee-uuu.*

Lyra had turned to the darkness ahead of us. "It is time," she said. "The enemy soon draws near."

"I will need your best support," Glorm told her. "**The village folk will not survive should we fall,** and I fear the Legion would share the same fate. Let us assist these novitiates and send this horde to the ninety-ninth realm." Brandishing his sword, he joined the elf in standing before the wall of inky gloom. "Today heralds the true return of a guild lost **aeons past. Today, the Crystal Owls** shall fly once more. . . ."

Today, I learned there were a bunch of reasons I wasn't made for dungeons. Here's the first one.

A small army of assorted shambling things. Say what you want about the **undead,** but they're a progressive people who welcome such things as diversity and multiculturalism. While villagers and Legionnaires bicker constantly over their many differences, the undead subtypes fight side by side—**zombies with green skin, revenants with blue.** I had no idea what skin color the things in front had. They were completely wrapped in bandages.

By the way, those were mummies.

There were many different types of shambling undead. Among them, mummies were the worst. Their touch inflicted **muffin rot,** an ancient magical disease. If not cured within the hour, your skin would begin to take on the color and texture of a poorly crafted wheat muffin.

(*Poorly crafted muffins are typically quite lumpy.*) Each hour after that would result in a permanent one-point reduction of all six attributes. It could be cured only by one specific potion, and if this disease were left to spread, you'd typically perish within a week (*give or take, depending on your vitality*).

What a day, right? Could things possibly get any worse? Allow me to rephrase that. We were **deep underground,** staring down an unliving horde, most of whom could inflict a hideous disease with a single touch, and the only thing between me and them was some creepy guy who was quite possibly a skeleton made of gold—*could things get any worse?*

My heart jumped as the mummy in front charged at me with one of those mitten-like bandaged hands. **Time almost froze,** and what was little more than a baker's mitt slowly flew toward my face. *No! Not muffin rot!! I look ridiculous enough as it is! Imagine how villagers would react if I returned to the surface looking like a crumbly brown pastry with lumps!*

In a total panic, I activated Dash, zooming back. No way was that thing touching me! **Back off, muffin hand!** Crazily enough, **the mummy Dashed forward toward me,** effectively countering my attempt at escape.

At that exact moment, it seemed that things had, in fact, gotten worse.

Then a stream of **brilliant light** came from behind me. The monster froze completely, its **diseased mitt** almost touching me.

Lyra had used her ult, **Castigate.**

It's a spell that calls upon **the power of Elune,** whoever that is. It harms only the unliving, blasting them with rays of golden light. Over half of the wave turned to ash, howling. Only the mummies withstood this power, their **"unliving energy"** far greater than all the others'. Still, they did not emerge unscathed. Three were turned to stone, including my assailant. The rest immediately ran, consumed by magical fear. Such is the power of Elune. *(Seriously, who is she?)*

The golden light dispersed.

Before me stood a statue, paw frozen in mid-attack.

I didn't get any XP here, since I didn't deal even a single point of damage. Quests, however, do not appear to work in the same manner. Thirteen undead were destroyed, and this number went toward my quest goal.

『A Call to Arms—Takedowns: 13/100 』

Wow. It really is that easy. I don't have to do anything. How do I claim that reward, though?

Before I could ask, the **ghostly bird** of Lyra's returned. It landed on her shoulder, chirped quietly into her ear, then faded from existence.

She turned to the gold knight. "**They're . . . not going to evacuate.** Kolbert is sending his best soldiers to assist us."

"Very well. Although I do not know how long we can hold. You will go OOM long before this ends."

*(OOM—that means "**out of mana**," mana being another word for energy. A **fancier** word. As expected of these two.)*

"I do have mana potions," the elf replied. "And there's that mana stone we . . ."

She trailed off as what I can only describe as a squishing sound came from up ahead. I steeled myself for the worst. Yet what appeared was the opposite of what I'd imagined. Instead of some **hideous aberration** with thousands of eyes was . . .

. . . ?

A <u>gelatinous</u> block
of pink and white ooze.

A basic level 1 monster. **A cake slime.**

Cake slimes had an average of 5 health, 0 armor, no abilities, and a **bite attack** that never resulted in more than 1 damage. Of all the varied monsters that could fight for the title of "**World's Noobiest,**" these guys would surely win.

Maybe that was why it did not seem all that interested in attacking us. Instead, it was sidling around us at a safe distance.

It . . . seems really scared. And not of us, but . . .

A second cake slime then appeared, followed by a third, a fourth, a fifth. **A whole herd of them.** Each of their forms quivered frantically as they slithered past with surprising speed.

"Look at those things **go**," I said. "Who knew slimes could move so f—"

A loud hiss cut me off, just like the one I'd heard earlier. Only, it was much louder this time—much closer—and up ahead came **scraping, slithering,** and two glowing yellow eyes—large eyes—high above, halfway to the ceiling.

Lyra cast the spell **Comet** to create a brilliant cube of magical light, illuminating the area ahead. And what this light revealed . . . !

Okay, first, I'm just going to ask you to prepare yourself. If, for example, you are currently consuming a food item, please take advantage of my warning and put said food item down before turning any more pages. I just don't want to receive angry letters from people who spit out half their cinnamuffin.

What we saw as the blue light spilled was . . .

a dragon.

It was a limbless subtype known as **a wyrm**—specifically a red wyrm—but it was still capable of spitting molten breath and chewing through my health like a freshly baked cocoa bean roll.

The **Halls of Agemmon** were, in fact, classified as a "**labyrinth**," the second-largest type of dungeon, and each labyrinth was supposed to have what's known as a "final guardian"—a boss of ominous presence and formidable strength. Normally, it would have remained on the lowest floor, in a kind of slumber, a guardian of ancient treasure. However, thanks to **Rite of Awakening** . . .

So Greyfellow was right.

It had crawled all the way from the labyrinth's depths, its movement speed far greater than all the rest.

The wyrm did not attack immediately, however. Its golden eyes seemed to analyze all of our stats. It hissed once more, and the stench that spilled from **its fang-filled maw was at least one tier above "boag."**

Lyra moved up behind the gold knight, slightly to his left. I took his right. Maybe it could be seen as cold of us to hide behind him, but Glorm had by far the most defense. **He was . . . our tank.**

"I assume it has **Flame Breath,**" the gold knight said.

"Yes, but it's going to open with **Devour.** Targeting him. Two seconds."

As she predicted, that maw came flying directly for me. But before I could even react, I was suddenly pulled to the left. Glorm had used **Telekinesis** to move me out of the way. With a sound of bent steel, at least fifty **swordlike fangs** came crashing to my right.

The wyrm pulled back with an annoyed snort.

I was now floating half a block above the floor, still under the effect of the gold knight's Telekinesis. With a wave of his hand, he sent me flying to the right. My arms and legs were hanging like a rag doll. I stopped directly in front of the wyrm.

"I will be using you as a shield," the gold knight said. "Given your **immunity,** you will, of course, be safe."

Safe?

"What kind of safety level are we talking about? Am I 'a little safe'? 'Safe enough'? 'Very' or maybe even **extremely safe**? I'd like to know before signing off on this."

Yeah, no amount of fire could hurt me, not even the ult of a **level 35 boss**. That didn't mean it wasn't scary. In addition to fire, fear washed over me. I dropped my sword and cried out, thrashing around, kicking the air.

"Remain still!" the gold knight hissed, **molten waves** sweeping past. "We're almost there!"

■■■ *"Do not resist,"* Lyra said. *She was behind us, using her telepathy.* *"He's not so good with magic. You could break the spell at any moment."*

Fine. I don't know how I calmed myself. I really, really don't.

Glorm was, of course, largely unharmed, and Lyra had moved just out of range.

When the flames finally stopped, the gold knight advanced. I advanced as well, **drifting forward like a floating puppet.**

The gold knight's blade also advanced *(into the beast's underbelly)*, and he swung endlessly. But these attacks did almost nothing to the enemy. At the rate its health was dropping—bit by bit, mere pixels—it would have taken hours. *(As a level 35 final guardian, or elite boss, the dragon had 6,000+ HP.)*

Glorm only stopped when the dragon reared back, and he hurled his **puppet-shield** in front of him. "It won't be so bad this time around," he said. "Flame Breath grows weaker with each subsequent use."

"That's comforting. Really."

However, the wyrm didn't use its **Flame Breath.** It paused, gold eyes glimmering. Then it gave a low snort. I somehow knew the beast was amused. *It knows,* I thought. Yeah, this was no moldsnout with −50 INT. **Dragons were filled with foul cunning,** as Kolbert once said. The monster had already realized breathing was pointless so long as the gold knight had his "shield."

There was a **metallic whine** as the wyrm moved, or shifted, too fast for a creature of that size. Down came that massive tail, with such speed it shattered the air, and there echoed the loudest sound:
GOW . . . !!

The gold knight waved me aside so that he took the blow. I was yanked back as he flew back fifteen blocks from the force of the attack, and I saw the amount of damage: −35. Enough to make a golem cry. But he did not shed a tear.

. . . ?! He barely took a scratch . . . !!

The gold knight, now beside Lyra, pulled me back farther like a bat on a leash.

"This would take an army," he said. "Our only hope is to delay. Perhaps when the Legion arrives, we—"

Suddenly, as though summoned by some spell, Zain rushed out of the gloom. *I know, right? Where'd he come from?!* He ran up to us, saw the wyrm, and just charged in, shouting. **A true hero!**

Sadly, most of his attacks only bounced off what must have been a **staggering amount** of armor.

The wyrm, instead of attacking, simply looked down at the young man with what could have been a smile.

*It's **enjoying** this,* I thought. *We're nothing to this thing, and it knows that.*

The Legionnaire just kept swinging. *"Ahh!!"* he cried.

"Clang!!" cried his sword.

"Haaaaa . . . !!"

"Clang! Clang!"

Against this opponent, he was little more than a **baby blockbird** furiously attacking with its beak.

"He appears to be under the effects of a **Berserk potion,**" Lyra said. *(Upon seeing an enemy, he could only attack.)*

"**Fool.**" Glorm was staring at Zain the same way he'd stared at me: analytically. "But I'll admit that he has skill for such a low level. **Yes, there is great potential within this novitiate, however abecedarian he may be. . . .**"

The elf nodded. "He will indeed be useful for **All That Follows.**"

"I suspect the same. Keep him alive, will you?" Glorm turned to me. "Stay within fifteen blocks. If the wyrm decides to reemploy its breath, I'll need to borrow you once more."

Then he rejoined the fight using that **ridiculous** spin move.

The dragon turned to him immediately, having grown bored of watching Zain. Again **its tail crashed down,** not on the golden armor but on a golden shield the gold knight had equipped. He wasn't knocked back at all this time.

Of course, there were times when **Glorm evaded** the dragon's attacks completely. Through Lyra's guidance, probably. But sometimes, he simply couldn't avoid that tail that swept endlessly from either side. When his health finally fell to half, the elf supported him with heals.

Just moments later, the rest of my friends arrived—the **Legion's finest,** along with some wolf guy in robes and a young man wearing what appeared to be . . . **armor made of leaves?** I had no idea who they were.

Extreme charged in like Zain before him. He'd chugged a **Berserk potion** as well. **The rest staggered forward, spellbound.**

Leo's jaw was about to hit the floor. "**What are they doing?! We can't fight that!**" Finally, he noticed me. "**Eeebs?!** What are you—why are you floating?!" Then he noticed Lyra. "Who is—" And he saw the gold knight, who was still **single-handedly tanking** the boss. "And who is—what's happening?!"

Kae took everything in with a few nods. "I think it's safe to say the option to evacuate Villagetown is still on the table."

"**On?** As of right now, it **is** the table," Lylla replied.

"No, the Legion never retreats," Hurion said. "Although, I **suppose** our code mentions nothing of **tactical displacement.** . . "

"Let's just go with **displacement,**" Steph said. "Not sure what's so tactical about running away screaming."

"Came here expecting the worst. Was not let down," Slach said. "And this is why I prefer being a pessimist."

"What's up with the skull guy?" Ched asked.

"What's up with **everything in front of me?!**" Becca added.

"Knew I shouldn't have given them those potions," Mooncloud said.

"Yeah, I say we grab those two noobs and bounce," Cobalt said. "This is a **Code Black.**"

"A Code Black? Really?" BlastLight gestured to Hurion. "You guys **do** remember that token of his, right?"

With this reminder, everyone suddenly began crowding around
Hurion, shouting and bumbling like villagers around the ice cream
stand when they're giving away free single-scoop cones.

"Do it!"

"Will you hurry up?!"

"Summon that **netherfreezing creature** already!"

Like before, Hurion concentrated while holding the white coin, and
the girl appeared, **all green with gossamer wings.**

Her eyes grew wide as she observed the dragon. "Wow! A red
wyrm! Last time I saw one of those things was during the **Battle of
Icehollow!**" Turning to Hurion, she flashed a smile. "**So.** Looks like
your party's in a bit of a jam."

Hurion did not mine around the vein. "**Request Assistance!!**"

Tossing away her sign, the faerie-like girl kept smiling. "**Oh, you
need some help, huh? You sure this time?**"

"Yes!!" Hurion shouted. Given how he'd always been so stoic before,
so calm and collected, the look on his face now was almost comical.
"**I'm sure! I'm very, very sure!!**"

"Hmm. Even so, I still think I should give you some time to think
about it. How does ten minutes sound?"

"There's no need! **I am absolutely, positively certain this time!**"

"Oh? But how am **I** to know? You've already called for me so many
times already."

Hurion pointed at the girl in sudden anger. "Redeem my wish, greenie, or I'll be calling you ten thousand more!"

"**Hmmph! Idiot!** Y'know, you're lucky there are laws that require me to follow through with your request! Because if it were up to me, I'd be summoning a rabbit!"

Still visibly irritated, she closed her eyes, as if focusing on a spell, while muttering to herself: "Insufferable **noobs!**" *(Her voice was fairly high-pitch, and that last word came out like a squeak.)*

Within seconds, the whole labyrinth shook violently, and not too far away appeared a vast pillar of white flame, inside of which arrived . . . **something.** Something impossibly huge. Even **Lyra's Comet** spell wasn't enough to fully illuminate the beast—that's how big it was.

The **wish girl** cast a Comet of her own to help out. Then she gasped, even cheered, no longer angry, apparently quite impressed by her own handiwork.

"Guys?! What's happening?!"

That was Zain, now backing away from the wyrm. It seemed his Berserk had worn off.

Extreme snapped out of it seconds later. "Huh. So Mooncloud was right. Chugging those potions was a **really bad idea.**"

But the rest of us weren't paying any attention. We were too busy staring at a monster twelve blocks high, our definition of **nightmare fuel** suddenly redefined.

"Um, I think I picked the right moment to show up."

"What . . . what . . . what . . . is . . . ?"

"I get the impression that **dragon** is going to take a beating."

"Very **relevant**, Nayte. Really very relevant."

"I don't know, but I'm sure it could **flatten** Villagetown."

"That's it. If I get out of this, I'm moving to the capital."

"Whoa!
I've never invoked anything like that! One of the gods must really want you to win! Um, on that note, he looks hungry. I suggest you stay far away from him. I mean, he's under your control and all, but you can't be too careful."

I don't really know what to call this jovial-looking fellow, so for now I will affectionately refer to him as . . . **Stompy.**

At first, the beast just stood there, almost motionless. "Give him a sec," the girl said. "He's got summoning sickness. It affects most living creatures. No matter how strong."

". . . W-what is that thing?!" Leo finally managed to shout/sputter.

"That happens to be a kaiju," said the wish girl. "His kind falls under the category of **greater being,** or unbelievably powerful creatures that reside in the far realms—the fifteenth or greater.

198

Cool, right?" She tilted her head. "Y'know, I'm pretty sure my grandfather used to hunt these guys. Their hide is used for some of the best leather armor."

"Your grandfather used to hunt things like **that?!** What level is **he?!**"

"One hundred, of course. **That's the maximum any human or demihuman can attain.** Err, I mean, people. You know. Like us. Monsters can go higher."

Upon noticing our new "ally," Glorm spun back to us and pulled Zain and Extreme to safety with Telekinesis. *(I dropped to the floor.)*

"Uwaaaaaaaa . . . !!"

(Thud.)

They landed in a heap at **Stompy's** feet. After they picked themselves up, it almost looked like they were about to charge back in.

Until they looked straight up.

The kaiju was moving at last. Looking down at them.

Hurion gave them a sidelong glance. "You're probably going to want to move."

200

The beast opened with **Breath of Magical Frost . . .** for 355 damage. You could feel the cold from here, see your breath. What followed was legendary. A battle between giants. Over and over, red scales clashed against black, and **huge sets of fangs** flew back and forth between torrents of ice and flame.

At one point, I saw Glorm raise an eyebrow. As in an eyebrow on his helmet/mask **actually moved.** "What level is that creature?" he asked Lyra. "I can't seem to Analyze it."

"Neither can I," she said. "None of my divinations are working."

Divinations are informational abilities, like **Analyze Monster.** The kaiju was so strong, so high level, that even Lyra—who clearly specialized in divination magic—couldn't see any of the monster's stats, not even a name. *(For those curious, her main class was Oracle. She was an information mage.)*

In a matter of minutes, the dragon's HP had fallen to half, while the other creature's health appeared to be regenerating.

It was over.
Only . . . it wasn't.

For behind the wyrm emerged at least a hundred other forms, either shambling or crawling. An army of mummies, crypt slimes, and undead owltrolls. Oh, and a few ice golems.

These were some of the **labyrinth's** other happy citizens. Originally positioned farther within, and with far less movement speed than a dragon, they had only now caught up.

Behind them all lurked a large black blob with a single huge eye and hundreds if not thousands of tentacles. A lurker, the same type of monster **Batwing** had mentioned some time ago.

*(By the way, **each one of these things**—being around level 35—had at least 100 HP. At least.)*

Of course, all of these creatures were not meant to be fought simultaneously. The labyrinth had been designed so that anyone crazy enough to attempt it would encounter one group at a time, where they could heal and recover and inch their way through, **battle after battle.** Fighting all of them at once was impossible. Even for a greater being from the fifteenth dimension.

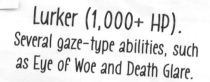

Lurker (1,000+ HP).
Several gaze-type abilities, such as Eye of Woe and Death Glare.

Ice golem
800+ HP; 100 STR;
AoE slow aura

Zombie troll
300+ HP; 150
STR; significant
physical damage

Crypt slime
100+ HP; melee attacks trigger acid
splash damage and a 250–500
durability loss to attacker's weapon,
depending on the material.

Mummy
200+ HP
75 STR

Despite having over 9,000 HP, the kaiju's **health bar** was noticeably shrinking as both the wyrm and lesser creatures attacked him.

Once, I saw him **Grab** an ice golem, which he then **Devoured** for 960 damage. He also **Stomped** a zombie troll for 720 and sent five mummies flying fifty or so blocks with a **Tail Sweep,** and at least twenty more fell to another **Frost Breath.**

Impressive, yes. It also counted toward my quest goal.

『A Call to Arms—Takedowns: 42/100 』

But no matter how many the beast **Stomped, Tail Swept, or Grabbed and Devoured,** just as many marched in to replace them.

Both Lyra and the wish girl moved in to support him, restoring slivers of his health with **Healing Tide** and shielding him from harm with **Power Shield.** But these spells were infinitesimal against the enemy's damage—what must have been 100+ DPS.

"Well, let's look on the bright side," BlastLight said. "At least he appears to be immune to muffin rot. There's that, right?"

When his health fell below half, the beast roared and used a different breath, one of brilliant green fire.

Many were consumed—a total of thirty-five, according to my VE.

『A Call to Arms—Takedowns: 77/100 』

But it just wasn't enough.

"He could really use our help," Becca said. "**Although** . . ."

Indeed—**although.** That's what the Legionnaires thought about going into that mess to help the poor monster.

Glorm turned to address us all. "I will commence with a frontal assault to distract some of their number. Those who wish to follow will be kept safe. If it becomes apparent that victory cannot be attained, you are to retreat, and Villagetown is to be evacuated. **Take the village folk to Ravensong**—follow the main road west, to the moon elf capital. There, they will be safe."

And just like that, he left a red trail as he charged in. Two swings drew the wyrm's wrath so that it was no longer focused on the kaiju. **Several mummies turned to him as well.**

Everyone was now looking to Kae and Hurion, who glanced at one another uncertainly.

"**Who is that guy?!**" Leo said. "He's one of us, but . . . **why is he talking like that? He sounds like some capital quest NPC!**"

"I think he took 'role-playing' a bit too far," Becca said.

"Yeah, that dude's minecart is definitely off its rails," Ched muttered. Then he sighed. "But I guess mine is, too." And he **Tumbled** forward, **unleashing a stream of bolts,** having finally equipped the goblin's crossbow from earlier. Kae turned to the others. "Ranged weapons, people. We'll try to kite."

Kite . . . ?

I stepped forward, about to say something heroic. Something like "I'd follow you guys into the **ninety-ninth dimension.**" But, sadly, all I was really able to say was . . . well, you know the sound a cat makes when it's really scared? A kind of *reeeeeeeeeerrrrr* sound? That was the sound I made as the gold knight "borrowed" me once more, so I could facetank some more dragon fire.

This time, he moved me almost directly in front of the dragon's maw, so that the flames, upon hitting my body, sprayed out in a wide cone. Glorm moved me closer and closer into its **Flame Breath, until I was practically inside of the thing's mouth.**

This, of course, totally startled the dragon. It just didn't know what to do. Still breathing, it backed up awkwardly, sputtering, its head turning every which way, **flames spraying harmlessly to either side.**

The whole time this went on, my friends used **ranged attacks** and **spells** on the closest enemies. This drew some of them away from the beast. Of course, none of my allies could stand toe to toe against any level 35 monster—and, really, who wants to deal with muffin rot or the acidic bite of a crypt slime?—so they continually backed up while **shooting/throwing/casting,** so that the monsters couldn't catch up to them—a strategy known as "**kiting.**"

Even though they were vastly out-leveled here and couldn't deal much damage, they could still serve as a distraction by **kiting the enemy around.**

CHOMP

"This is really getting old."

Tail Sweep

The wolf man—called **Faolan**—summoned several small ice slimes to impede the enemy's movement and distract them further. The one in leaf armor, Nayte, used **Frost Shot** to imbue his arrows with magical frost, reducing the enemy's movement speed (by 25%). The others used whatever ranged weapons they had, from small bows to throwing knives, shuriken. A few were throwing flasks of **Holy Water,** a type of splash potion that harms only the undead.

Soon, at least half of the horde began funneling toward **Team Ranged.** They completely ignored Lyra, the wish girl, the gold knight, and me, flowing past us like a monster river. This relieved enough pressure from Stompy so that he could keep dumpstering things.

To further slow their progress, Faolan used the spell **Ice Web** to **create areas of frost on the ground.**

And even though my friends couldn't deal that much damage individually, when all seventeen focused on the same target, that target fell in less than ten seconds—**a strategy called . . . focusing.** *(Shocking, I know.)*

Bladestorm:
Throws up to 25 daggers (or shuriken) from inventory. All weapons used for this ability are then destroyed.

Ice Web:
Conjures a 5 × 5 web of magical frost. Any creature in this zone is slowed by 80% while inside and for three seconds after leaving.

Holy Water

Notice the frozen feet.

Frost Shot:
Imbues your next ranged attack with magical frost, causing +25% damage and slowing your target by 25% for three seconds.

Triple crossbow

They dropped around fifty mummies in the next several minutes.

That entire time, the kaiju worked on the remaining mummies while the gold knight continued to tank the boss by himself using a lot of potions and occasional support from Lyra.

Then, just before the Legionnaires returned, **the dragon pulled a really tricky move.** It went to breathe again, so the gold knight threw me in front. But the boss canceled its Flame Breath before the ability activated—and instead **hit me with its tail.** Dragons really are that smart.

Lyra hit me with **Power Shield** just before the **Tail Sweep** landed. I still went flying, though, some thirty blocks into the dark expanse.

Well, the dragon's **Flame Breath** was weak at this point, so now Glorm was able to withstand it just using his shield. He was okay. As for me . . .

I'd landed right next to an advancing wave of crypt slimes. A vast herd moving like an ocean. You couldn't believe how many. And you couldn't believe just how fast those things were moving. The sight of an **actual slime stampede** left me totally stunned. Even as my friends called out some distance away, telling me to run, **I simply stood there, frozen.**

But one voice seemed much closer than all the rest—"**Move, idiot!**"—along with the sound of fluttering wings.

"You're such a nerb."

"What's a ner— **Hey!** One of those things just jumped at me!"

"Y'know, I really shouldn't get involved like this."

"Yeah, why help us? It's probably smarter to let the entire village get stampeded by **angry, acidic** slimes. That makes sense."

"Well, I'm not supposed to provide direct assistance. I'm gonna get in so much **trouble** for this. I just know it."

Yeah, that weird girl saved me. *(We still don't know her name.)*

Within seconds, we landed on top of Stompy's head. He didn't seem to mind as he continued his rampage through the rest of the horde. When he went to use his breath, we steadied ourselves by grabbing his horns.

211

"Can't **believe** I'm doing this," the girl muttered, while glancing down at the rapidly approaching slime ocean. "Hmm. Suppose there's only one real way to deal with a herd like that. Luckily for you guys, I just learned a new crowd-pleaser and threw **a ton of points** into it."

"What's a cr—"

There was the loudest roar as a **fiery cube** flew from the girl's outstretched hands, leaving a **trail of sparks and thick gray smoke**, until it finally exploded in a boxy pattern.

(Would you be surprised if I told you the name of that spell was Firecube?)

"Are they like, taking applications for **Wizard School**, or . . . ?"

The radius of that blast was **unreal.**

I'm kind of confused, though, because that crowd certainly didn't look too pleased. The few slimes that survived ran away.

The lurker ran away, too, with a hideous shriek *(lurkers are afraid of fire)*. It couldn't do much, anyway. Most of its attacks came in the form of "gaze" abilities, which it tried using on **Glorm** a few times, but his armor actually repelled or reflected them like a mirror.

This time, it really was over.

The wolf man, Faolan, having returned to the battle, used his ultimate spell, **Boreal Blast,** summoning a blizzard of epic proportions, blinding, slowing, and damaging the thirty or so mummies that remained. They couldn't do anything.

For Stompy, what now stood before him was little more than a great deal of ice cream that he only had to **Grab and Devour.**

Soon enough, the only thing left was the final guardian, which Stompy began tearing through with renewed vigor.

As if that wasn't enough, Glorm used his ult, **Blade of Retribution.** A hole formed in the ceiling, through which fell rays of golden light and a gigantic sword of . . . blinding red energy.

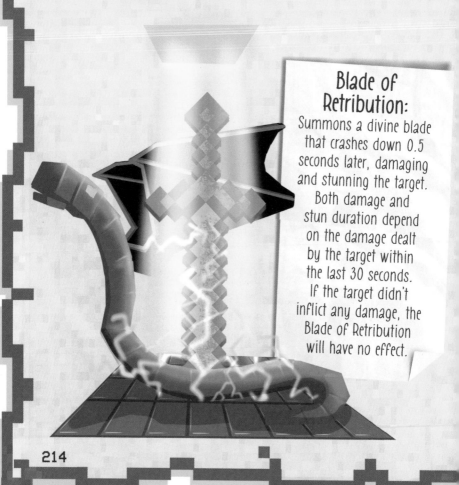

Blade of Retribution:
Summons a divine blade that crashes down 0.5 seconds later, damaging and stunning the target. Both damage and stun duration depend on the damage dealt by the target within the last 30 seconds. If the target didn't inflict any damage, the Blade of Retribution will have no effect.

I wasn't even surprised after everything I'd seen so far.

It assisted the final guardian in achieving a most peaceful state of 0 health.

The **winged girl** set me down on the labyrinth floor about the same time the dragon fell. The last thing I remember here is crystals, so many, **a mountain of them, an ocean of them,** flying **into everyone around me.** There must have been twenty or thirty thousand, fifty thousand, I don't know, each crystal part of the dragon's or some lesser being's life energy, the green ones worth 100 XP, the whites 500, and the blues 10,000.

A pile of items sprang up where the dragon had been, like a fountain, along with so many dragon **scales,** dragon **bones,** dragon **horns,** dragon **teeth,** dragon **leather.** And from the wings? There were a bunch of gold boxes called pocket stables, which could hold animals like flasks hold water. It's an easy way to put away your ride, like a horse, for example. There was also a shard of metal much like the one I saw in **Lavacrest.** This drew the gasps of many. **It was a piece of Kolbert's sword.**

From somewhere in my mind, a cold male voice rang:

〖 *The labyrinth Halls of Agemmon has been cleared. The following rewards have been bestowed upon all participants. Dragon Affinity: You have absorbed part of a dragon's soul, allowing you to level up any class related to . . .* 〗

215

The voice said a lot of other stuff, but I wasn't listening, and everyone around me was shouting and screaming, just totally freaking out, and as hundreds of crystals kept flying into my body, I staggered back and collapsed, unable to move or think. . . .

"Hey!" I heard Leo say. "What's his problem?!"

Others paid no attention to me, instead shoveling the countless dragon items into their inventories. "We can ask Breeze to borrow that forge from Runt," Hurion said to Kae. "Her father has that recipe book. Maybe we can try figuring out how to craft dragon scale armor?"

That was it.

What followed was darkness, silence. It felt as though I slept for a very long time.

When I woke up, I was curled up in my bed in the **Lost Keep.**

And I was back to my old self, a cat, no longer "anthropomorphic." The **Wildshape** potion was no longer in effect.

I sat up. Yawned. Looked around my empty room. **Breeze wasn't there,** but I was in her room. Strangely, everything that had happened before felt so **distant and surreal.** Like a dream I'd had weeks ago.

Could it be? Was all of that just some really strange dream . . . ?

The door opened. I jumped so high it would have been easy to mistake me for a mage who'd cast the spell Fly, as the person currently standing before me was none other than—

"Breeze . . . ?!"

"Morning," she said, cheerfully—too cheerfully. Along with the way she smiled, it was as though nothing had actually happened. Of course nothing had happened! Something so ridiculous as muffin rot could **only be the product of my feral imagination!**

I felt the **biggest wave of relief.** "I had the **craziest** dream," I said. "First, you left me alone in the middle of the night, and **I needed to go to the Lost Keep! Then there was an attack! Goblins! Pigmen with blue skin!** And I followed one into the mine tunnels, right, only to discover the real threat. Tons of stuff from this massive dungeon. **A labyrinth,** it was called. There was this **huge red** dragon, and mummies, and acid slimes, ice golems. Oh, and a lurker, too! Then the Legion used Wish to summon this huge dragon thing, and, and . . ."

Something caught my eye. In the corner of my vision, slowly blinking, was the following:

『 Level Up 』

"What does that . . . so all of that . . . it really . . ."

When Breeze continued, her voice sounded far away: "Seems you experienced some type of fatigue from gaining so much XP in such a short amount of time. I assume it's because you were level 0."

"Were . . . ?!"

When I opened my screen, the amount of XP I had was unbelievable: **258,850.**

I was now level 14. I only had to choose which class—**or classes**—to level up. Of course, even something so simple as thinking was a difficult task at this point. I pushed classes aside for now.

By the way, the quest the gold knight shared, "A Call to Arms," had completed automatically. Yeah, 2,500 XP was nothing compared to what I earned from that labyrinth. Still, eight hundred emeralds were now safely stashed in my inventory. They'd apparently teleported there somehow. Was that part of the quest's magical contract?

"So the village is okay," I said. "It's . . . still standing."

Breeze nodded. "We took down their leader. Well, the one in charge of the surface attack. But that was nothing compared to what you saw."

"Yeah. **It was total insanity.** What's a dungeon like that doing below Villagetown, anyway?!"

"**Shh! Not so loud, huh?**" That was Kolbert, stepping inside. He looked exhausted, and his armor had seen better days. "Her father doesn't want anyone knowing what happened in the labyrinth. Especially the dragon. Most of the villagers think **the Prophecy** isn't real. **If they knew the truth, we'd be facing a total panic situation.** So if anyone asks, you just returned from a hunt, and there was no dragon, got it?"

"Fine." When I looked at Breeze again, I was reminded of something. "Wait. How about Runt? Is he back, too?"

"Yeah, he's here," Kolbert said. "Luckily, he brought some **Knights of Aetheria** who really helped out—ah. See ya, Eeebs. And remember what I said! A hunt!"

This last part I barely heard as I was zooming out of my room. "**And no dragon! None!**"

Well, the village was still intact. *(Somewhat.)* It had clearly suffered a lot of damage in the surface attack, but everywhere I went, people were carrying around blocks. It was already being rebuilt.

I spent the next several minutes asking these people about . . .

"**Runt?** Yeah, he's around here."

"Just saw him, hurrr. I think he went to check on the school."

"**Noobery!** I'm a **Knight of Aetheria,** not some tour guide! Go ask someone else!"

"Hurrrrrrrr! Get away from me! Can't you see my shop was just blown up?! **Oh, my muffins! My scones! All burned . . . !!**"

I ran into Leaf, who was shouting in the street: "Two layers of spellforged steel, melted! How is that even possible?! That was **spellforged steel . . . !!**"

Extreme, standing next to him, gave him a tired look. "**Will you stop saying that?!**"

Leaf glared at him. "Yeah, I'm sure you're quite happy about what happened to my shop! And yours is still standing! How strange!" Then he noticed me. "Hey! It's **him!** That **blue thing!** He stole some of my best weapons! **Get back here, thief!**"

I just kept running. At last, I nearly ran into Runt. **I knew it was him.** Like Breeze, **he had a kind of aura;** there was just something about him that I can't explain.

I ran right up to him. And realized I had no idea what to say. So I opened with a "hi."

He said nothing, just stared down at me in an absent way. Then, with a sigh, he simply walked off.

I tried talking to him several more times throughout the day, but every time he just avoided me. **Well, I wasn't going to give up.** I came all this way for him. He'd talk. **I'd follow him around singing until he talked!** But I stopped when I heard a voice coming from the shadow of an alley.

"Let him be for now," Lyra said. "He will talk to you when he's ready."

"Let him be for now," I repeated flatly, approaching her. **"Really?! I'm partly here because of him!"**

The humanoid wolf, Faolan, appeared from the shadows. "He is far from being the only reason. In truth, there are hundreds you will assist."

Behind him emerged the gold knight, green eyes glowing.

Once more, I gave them an exasperated look. **"Will someone just tell me what I'm supposed to be doing?!"**

"We will," Glorm said. "There is much a kitten must learn. And not nearly as much time." He turned into the alley. It was really dark there. "But not here. **If you will be so kind as to follow me."**

221

They took me to Kolbert's house.

He was there, along with Kae.

"You can learn **monster skills**, right?" Kolbert asked.

"Yes?"

"Well, I think there's a reason for that." He gestured to Kae. "Try to teach him something. Like **Aspect of the Spider.**"

"How do I do that?"

"Stand in front of him and think about it really hard?"

"Okay."

So I did exactly as instructed. It took several minutes of intense concentration, but eventually, **a well of ghostly white light formed around me.** Motes of the same color flittered around in the air. These cubes of light drifted lazily toward the Legionnaire and flew into him.

He staggered back.

"It actually worked?!"

He started effortlessly climbing the wall, just like a spider.

"No way!"

I'd just taught Kae an ability. And not just any ability, but one only monsters of the "**insect**" subtype normally have access to.

"That is your main purpose here," Lyra said. "**You serve as a link**

between monster and man. Using your gift, you will be able to grant a wide variety of powers to Aetherian and Terrarian alike."

"Wait a minute." I opened my status screen—to the abilities subsection.

You can guess what I'd learned. **Tail Sweep. Flame Breath.** Just like with the goblin, I'd somehow absorbed them.

"So he's like some kind of boss," Kae said. "Or he will be. Once he levels up and throws more points into all that stuff. And then he can teach all of that to **us**." He paused, clearly struggling as much as I was at this new revelation. "He's like . . . our own personal **trainer NPC,** except for monster-only stuff. That's . . . really cool."

Once more, the gold knight gave me an analytical look. "Indeed, he will be of great use for '**All That Follows.**' The return of the **Red Star** coincides with a time of great sorrow for all of Aetheria, yet **with this kitten we will have a fighting chance.** The descendants of past heroes may be trained to a degree that rivals their ancestors. Once he trains Breeze, **I almost fear to imagine what that girl will then be capable of** . . . and of course, the one known as Runt will not be too far behind."

"We must remain cautious even so," Lyra said. "For no matter how powerful they become, the enemy will always be stronger."

"Certainly. Which reminds me . . ." The gold knight looked at me. "I see that you have a tellstone in your possession. May I borrow it?"

"Um, yeah," I said, wondering why he didn't have one. "Here."

"What poor craftsmanship," he said, inspecting it. "I'm surprised it functions at all. . . ."

Soon, an image appeared in the stone. That of **EnderStar,** standing in the middle of an onyx chamber with two large braziers burning low. He pointed at a group of bramblemanes in deep violet robes, and with a crackle his voice resounded from the stone, "**Fools! Neophytes! Unintelligible uninitiates! How many times can you fail?!**"

And with a **great thrashing** he knocked over one brazier. He then grabbed the other brazier and swung it wildly at a rune chamber, at a wall, and, finally, at a golem—an adamant golem. When his attack resulted in 0 damage, he zapped it with a stream of green lightning until the golem glowed bright red and melted into pixels. He then muttered something about "**calling the enderhurgles.**"

His underlings had already slowly backed away and were now running into some portal one had created through some spell. **The portal then winked out of existence.**

EnderStar moved—to cast a spell, perhaps—then paused abruptly; he turned to face the tellstone. In a blink, all you could see on the stone's surface was a **large violet eye glowing** with **sheer rage and malevolence.** He was looking directly at us.

Clink.

The stone cracked. The image faded.

The gold knight turned to Lyra. "Perhaps we should have first checked on S. We have not heard from him for some time."

"He will be fine," the elf said. "He's with Pebble, now."

The rest of my friends piled in seconds later.

"I made a stack of cinnamuffins."

"Do you think that girl could teach me how to cast Firecube?"

"Hi, Eeebs. So it looks like you've returned to cat form."

"Hey, um . . . that was some good tanking. And thanks for the crossbow."

"You like Cobalt's new hair? I just helped him dye it."

"Don't worr[y] Eeebs. We'll h[elp] you sort o[ut] your classe[s]"

"You'll wanna read this. It has info on classes, abilities . . ."

"Amber and I are gonna open a shop specializing in dragon stuff. Cool, huh? We're also gonna level up Dragoon. It's a class that lets you have a dragon companion. And dragon abilities. We just really like dragons."

"Um, you can put your weapons away, **noob**."

"Can someone tell me why Kae is on the ceiling?"

"Yeah, okay. After what happened at the opera house, I almost want to glue these things to my hands."

Before long, I was **bombarded** with promises. They all wanted to help me with my spells and skills.

"What's going on out there?!" It was the winged girl.

She's still here?!

She emerged from a back room with a half-eaten **cinnamuffin** in one hand. "Dude. These things are so good, like so good." She sighed. "I've gotta say: I'd really missed this realm."

Kolbert, after giving her a blank look, turned to Glorm. "What's **she still** doing here?"

She flew up to him. "I'll have you know **I just got fired** from a very nice job so all of you can keep trying to 'save the world.' A little respect might be in order, huh?!" Then she turned to me and smiled. "Oh, hey, nerb. **Glad you survived.** I mean, if you really **can** do what they say you can, you're kinda one of the most important . . . err, **people** in the world. Of course, you still have plenty to learn. So that's why we'll be heading for Silverfall in a few days. We're gonna help you get up to speed on **everything.**"

I blinked. "Silverfall . . . ?"

"A moon elf city," Kolbert said. "It's on the coast, not too far from where Runt and Breeze are headed. You'll be able to visit them easily."

"Such a beautiful place," the girl said. "Haven't been there in forever. Oh." She extended a hand. "Sorry. **I'm Nelmi.**"

In any case, that's about it. Soon, I'd be going to go to this town called Silverfall with a bunch of strangers. I'd learn more there. Yet I'd already learned so much. So, just like that, I was supposed to teach people stuff they couldn't normally learn. Like how to move like a spider or even how to breathe fire like a dragon. I was going to be the best teacher **the Overworld** had ever known. Not bad, huh?

While everyone was talking about the kind of things I could eventually teach them, someone knocked on the door.

It was Emerald and Breeze. Both had on new gear. And **something about Breeze seemed different,** but I couldn't say what.

They both looked at Glorm and Nelmi, then exchanged a look.

Then Breeze smiled. "**What did we miss?**"

Cube Kid is the pen name of Erik Gunnar Taylor, a writer who has lived in Alaska his whole life. A big fan of video games—especially Minecraft—he discovered early that he also had a passion for writing fan fiction. Cube Kid's unofficial Minecraft fan fiction series, *Diary of a Wimpy Villager*, came out as e-books in 2015 and was immediately met with great success in the Minecraft community. They were published in France by 404 éditions in paperback and now return in this same format to Cube Kid's native country under the title *Diary of an 8-Bit Warrior*. When not writing, Cube Kid likes to travel, putter with his car, devour fan fiction, and play his favorite video game.

Diary of an 8-Bit Warrior

Diary of an 8-Bit Warrior:
From Seeds to Swords

Diary of an 8-Bit Warrior:
Crafting Alliances

Diary of an 8-Bit Warrior:
Path of the Diamond

Diary of an 8-Bit Warrior:
Quest Mode

Diary of an 8-Bit Warrior:
Forging Destiny

Tales of an 8-Bit Kitten:
Lost in the Nether

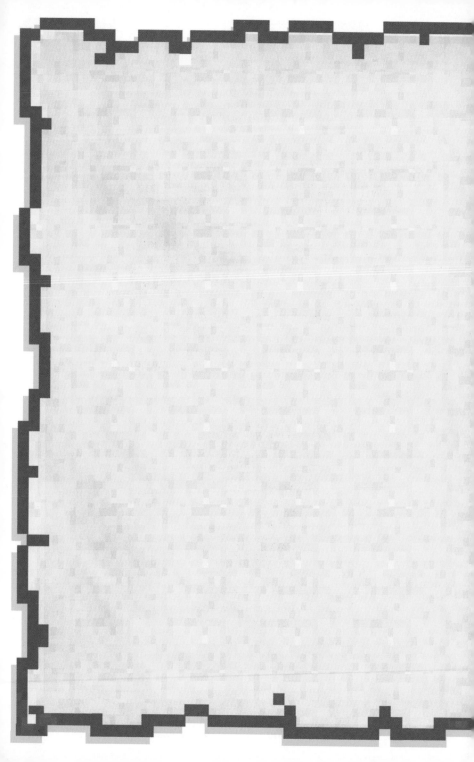